Lottie's Courage

A Contraband Slave's Story

Phyllis Hall Haislip

By

Phyllis Hall Haislip

*Follow your dreams
wherever they may be.
Nice meeting you,
Sincerely,
C— King*

W M KIDS WHITE MANE KIDS

SHIPPENSBURG, PENNSYLVANIA

This White Mane Books publication
was printed by
Beidel Printing House, Inc.
63 West Burd Street
Shippensburg, PA 17257-0708 USA

The acid-free paper used in this book meets the guidelines for permanence and durability of the Committee on Production Guidelines for Book Longevity of the Council on Library Resources.

For a complete list of available publications
please write
White Mane Books
Division of White Mane Publishing Company, Inc.
P.O. Box 152
Shippensburg, PA 17257-0152 USA

Library of Congress Cataloging-in-Publication Data

Haislip, Phyllis Hall.
　　Lottie's courage : a contraband slave's story / by Phyllis Hall Haislip.
　　　p. cm.
　　Summary: In 1862, a ten-year-old girl and an old woman start a new life after they escape a slave trader and are rescued by Union soldiers, who take them as "contraband of war" to Fortress Monroe in Hampton, Virginia.
　　ISBN 1-57249-311-9 (alk. paper)
　　　1. Virginia--History--Civil War, 1861-1865--Juvenile fiction. [1. Virginia--History--Civil War, 1861-1865--Fiction. 2. Slavery--Fiction. 3. African Americans--Fiction. 4. Mothers and daughters--Fiction. 5. Missionaries--Fiction. 6. United States--History--Civil War, 1861-1865--Fiction.] I. Title.

PZ7.H128173 Lo 2002
[Fic]--dc21

2002073569

Dedication

In memory of my mother,
Loretta Dunn Hall (1908–1997)

Motherless Child

Sometimes I feel like a motherless child,
Sometimes I feel like a motherless child,
A long way from home,
A long way from home.

Sometimes I feel like a motherless child,
Sometimes I feel like a motherless child,
Sometimes I wish I could fly, like a bird in the sky,
Sometimes I wish I could fly, like a bird in the sky,
Little closer to home.

Motherless children have a real hard time,
Motherless children have a such a real hard time,
So long, so long, so long,
Sometimes I feel like a motherless child,
Sometimes I feel like a motherless child,
So far away.

Sometimes I feel like freedom is near,
Sometimes I feel like freedom is near,
But we're so far away,
Sometimes I feel like it's close at hand,
Sometimes I feel like freedom is near,
But we're so far from home.

Sometimes, sometimes, sometimes,
So far, so far, so far,
So far Mama from you, so far.

Traditional African American Spiritual

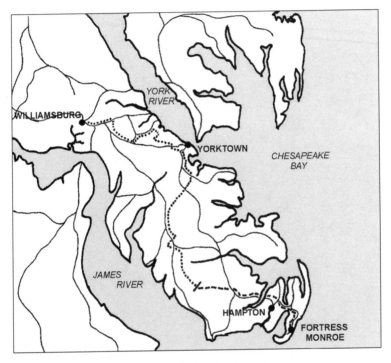

The Virginia Peninsula

For Lottie, the twenty-nine miles that separated
Williamsburg from Fortress Monroe became the
difference between slavery and freedom. The dotted line
shows her painful journey. On the lower peninsula, she
came under the Union army's protection and proceeded
to Fortress Monroe as a contraband of war.

Courtesy of Otis L. Haislip, Jr.

Contents

Contents

Acknowledgments

The help and support of many people have made this work possible. My son, Alex, and my neighbor, Gerry Poriss, read and criticized the first draft. Jane Ashworth, Barbara Ball, Mary Louise Clifford, and Sara Puccini of the James River Writers' Group gave me help and support throughout the writing process. Agnes King had faith in the project and encouraged me to keep working on it. Hope Yelich at The College of William and Mary and David Johnson at Casemate Museum assisted me with the illustrations. Jan Gilliam of the Abby Aldrich Rockefeller Folk Art Museum at Colonial Williamsburg steered me to Roddy Moore, the director of the Blue Ridge Institute and Museum, who advised me on the correct kind of doll for the story. My husband, Otis, has provided technical help on the manuscript and the illustrations. More importantly, he regularly performed KP duty at home in order to give me time to write.

Chapter 1
Sold!

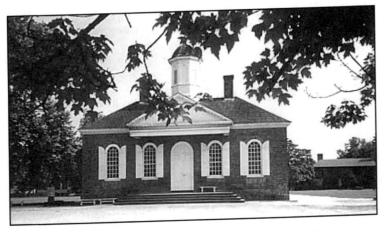

Williamsburg Courthouse, built in 1770, where Lottie was sold in 1862

Author's Photograph

Lottie stood on the auction block in her faded, blue-gingham dress, her legs trembling. Several hundred people milled around Market Square near the Williamsburg Courthouse for the annual New Year's Day slave auction. The auctioneer pounded his gavel for silence. He was a stocky, tired-looking man with a flushed face, and he seemed eager to get the day's business concluded. When the crowd quieted, he began the sale, "This chocolate-colored girl looks small, but she's almost ten years old. She has helped in the kitchen and in the stables." He turned to Lottie. "Stand up straight and turn around so everyone can see you." Lottie straightened her slumped shoulders and slowly turned around. The day was cold, and Lottie felt exposed, almost naked with everyone looking at her. She heard a catcall from someone in the crowd. She felt her face go hot with the shame of being looked over as if she were an animal for sale.

"It says here," the auctioneer read from a paper in a raspy voice, "that she can milk cows, churn butter, and take care of chickens." He paused for a moment to clear his throat before he continued. "Although she's not used to hard work, she's still young enough to be broke to field work. The bidding opens at four hundred dollars."

Lottie bit her bottom lip when she heard the words, "broke to field work." She had seen the drudgery of slaves hoeing tobacco all day in the hot sun, and she knew their lives were short and miserable. With those awful words echoing in her head, Lottie searched the crowd for her mother, wondering if she had heard the auctioneer. Lottie's gaze fell on the powder magazine. Beyond it was Francis Street, where she had lived her whole life. Now she wished she could run, run back to the only home she had ever known. A hand went up as the buyers began bidding.

"Four hundred twenty-five dollars," offered a tall man wearing a slouch hat.

"Four fifty." The bid came from somewhere near the back of the crowd.

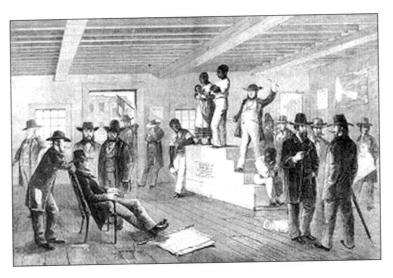

Slave auction in Virginia, 1861

The Illustrated London News, February 16, 1861;
courtesy of *The Illustrated London News* Picture Library

"Four seventy-five," the first man called out. Then there was silence. For a fleeting second, Lottie hoped that no one was going to buy her.

"Sold!" the auctioneer said, pounding his gavel amid a stream of rapidly spoken words, "to Mr. Slye for four hundred seventy-five dollars." Just then Lottie spotted her mother as she slowly made her way through the crowd.

"Come down from there, girl," the auctioneer said, shuffling his papers to prepare for the next sale. "We haven't got all day."

Lottie kept her mother in view as she stepped shakily down from the block. The last slave to be auctioned was a stooped, white-haired man, and he shuffled to the block, mumbling quietly to himself. Lottie felt numb. She had been sold. Sold to a man she didn't know. What would happen to her now?

Mama's sorrow-filled face grew closer. Lottie stooped and picked up her oversized woolen coat from where it lay on the steps of the courthouse and struggled into it.

"This way." Slye, the man who bought her, roughly grabbed her arm. Lottie flinched at the man's touch. He was evil looking with sunken cheeks, gray whiskers, and one dead eye. He steered her toward a group of slaves standing near one corner of the brick courthouse.

Lottie went off with the man, away from her approaching mother. She craned her neck to make sure her mother was following. She stumbled, and Slye shook her. "Pay attention to where you're going," he growled, fixing his cold eye on her.

They approached an older man with lanky hair, wearing a dark coat, shiny with grease. A shotgun rested in the crook of his arm. He was guarding other recently purchased slaves. A small group of onlookers, mostly slaves, stood nearby.

"She's the last, Ferris," Slye told the other man, giving Lottie a shove in his direction. "Let's get these people secured and get going."

Lottie saw Mama limp toward her. She wasn't wearing a coat, and the apron she had put on this morning before preparing the major's breakfast was still tied around her waist. Lottie guessed that her mother had left her work without permission. Before anyone could stop her, Mama gathered Lottie in her arms. "It'll be all right," Mama said quietly, trying to comfort Lottie before someone forced them apart. "It'll be all right."

"What will happen to me, Mama?" Lottie asked, her words thick with dread.

"I don't know," Mama whispered, wondering if she'd ever see her daughter again. She had hoped that Lottie would find a new owner in Williamsburg. Now that hope was gone. She probably would be taken south to work in the cotton fields of the Carolinas where she would become one of the expendable work horses of farm life. Her little girl would be old before her time, if she survived the harsh life of unending toil. Lottie's mother struggled to keep her voice steady. "I heard someone say you'd been bought by...," she choked on the hated words, "a slave trader."

Slave trader. Lottie had heard about slave traders. She bit her bottom lip. There was no need for bogey men to scare slave children in Virginia. The words "slave trader" were enough to frighten the bravest child.

"Am I being sold south?" Lottie asked, remembering stories she had heard of her father's uncertain fate.

"I don't know, child," said Mama, her gentle face full of pain. "There's no telling where you'll end up. But you need to remember where I'll be. In Winchester, at Mrs. Emma Howell's. Say it."

"Winchester, Mrs. Emma Howell's," Lottie repeated the words as she had so many times in the last several days. Mama had worried what would happen to them ever since their owner, Mrs. Shadwell, died in childbirth last October. Major

Shadwell had been away fighting with the Confederate army and had returned home ten days ago. The day after Christmas he told Mama the dreadful news that she had been inherited by her former mistress's sister in Winchester and Lottie was to be sold.

The auction was over, and the crowd was beginning to disperse. Lottie heard the clank of chains as Slye began fitting iron collars around the necks of the seven men and boys. He then fastened a long chain through the hasp of the padlocks that held the neck irons, chaining the men together in a line. Lottie glanced at the other slaves, hoping she might see a familiar face. But she recognized no one.

The man called Ferris began tying the women with a rope. "Out of the way," he said to Mama, pushing her aside when it was Lottie's turn to be tied with the others. As Mama watched helplessly, he fastened a rope halter around Lottie's neck and attached her to the heavy-set, older woman behind her. Whenever the other women moved, the rope chafed Lottie's neck. She bit her lip again. She had seen slaves traveling through Williamsburg in similar slave coffles, but she had never imagined how wretched it would feel.

Slye turned to Ferris, "Let's get going," he said. "We've a way to go before nightfall."

Mama hugged Lottie one last time. "Be strong. Only the strong survive," she said. "I want you to promise you'll be strong."

In spite of her brave words, Mama looked so defeated that for a moment Lottie feared more for her mother than for herself. "I'll be strong," Lottie said, trying to sound confident. "I'll survive."

As a slave Lottie's mother had been taught to hide her feelings, and she had hidden them so often these last several days, they had formed a great knot in her chest. Now Lottie's words loosened the knot, and she began to sob.

Ferris and Slye mounted up. Then Ferris prodded the slave at the head of the coffle with the end of his gun. "Move on," he barked.

The line started with a stumble and jerk. The rope cut into Lottie's neck. For a moment, she choked. Mama let go of her, and she got in step with the others, easing the tension on her neck. As the slaves began to move away, Mama thrust into Lottie's hands the flax tow sack she had packed the night before.

The coffle made its way down Duke of Gloucester Street. Lottie heard her mother's sob-racked voice raised above the commotion of departure. "Gone! All gone! Everyone I've ever loved is gone. Why doesn't God just kill me? It isn't right to take my child. It isn't right. It isn't right."

Lottie painfully turned to catch one last glimpse of Mama. Slye saw her waver in line. His whip whizzed through the air. It burned her shoulders through her coat, and its tail bit into the side of her face. The tears Lottie had been stifling all morning spilled over as she staggered forward, her face burning and her heart breaking. "Oh, Mama, Mama," she sobbed. "Will I ever see you again?"

Chapter 2
Motherless Child

Detail of an illustration showing a slave coffle

Library of Congress, Prints and Photographs Division [LC-USZ62-2574]

The slave coffle moved sluggishly down the deeply rutted road. Lottie had never been out of Williamsburg, and each step took her farther away from home and Mama. She trudged into the wind, head down, barely able to put one foot ahead of the other. Her heart seemed to have dropped into her feet, and her feet felt like the heavy flatirons Mama used to press the major's shirts. She picked up and put down each foot precisely as she had seen Mama do with the hot flatirons. If she kept a steady pace, the rope did not burn her neck.

She walked and walked through the desolate January countryside with its naked trees and gray deserted fields. She passed small farms with outbuildings in need of paint and went through a village that was no more than a general store and an ordinary. Occasionally, someone went by them on horseback or in a farm wagon. Most white folks turned their heads and did not look. Other slaves gazed at them sadly. As Lottie toiled along, she kept track of Slye. He rode beside the coffle, constantly fingering his whip. It fell on anyone who faltered.

After what seemed liked hours, Slye called a halt, and Lottie and the others dropped on a stretch of pine straw-covered ground. Lottie loosened the brown leather shoes she had gotten new at Christmas. Her feet felt swollen and blistered.

"Are you all right, child?" the woman behind Lottie whispered.

Lottie turned and looked up into a round, kind face, framed with white hair captured in a red kerchief. The woman was wearing more than one shawl, wrapped tightly about her. The outermost shawl was purple and black wool, and the woman had gold hoops in her ears. Lottie nodded.

"Don't take those off," the woman warned, pointing to Lottie's shoes. "You won't get them back on. Then you'll really be in for it."

Lottie tried to make herself comfortable on the cold, damp ground, grateful for the chance to rest. She opened the tow bag Mama had given her. She swallowed with difficulty when she saw Bebe, the rag doll, Mama had made her long ago. She gently stroked the doll's black face with its embroidered smile, longing to touch it to her own. Beside her doll were buttermilk biscuits that Mama had wrapped in a worn, linen napkin. Beneath Bebe and the biscuits was the piece of cloth Mama had received at Christmas. Lottie had loved the bright fabric with its pink roses as soon as she had seen it, and Mama, having so little to give her, had put the material into the bag instead of an extra shift. Tears smarted in Lottie's eyes and she sniffled, trying to pull herself together.

The white-haired woman heard the sniffling. She looked sadly at the huddled figure of the frightened, delicate-looking girl clinging to the pitiful remnants of her other life. One of the thick braids that had been pinned to the girl's head had come unpinned, and the hairpins were falling out. "My name's Louisa, but everybody calls me Weza," she said. "What's yours?"

Lottie wiped her eyes on her sleeve. She struggled with the pain in her chest. She had heard of heartbreak, but she had not realized until today that a person's heart actually felt like there was something pressing down on it, crushing it. "I'm Lottie," she said with great effort.

"That's a good sounding name," said Weza. Her voice conveyed reassurance and approval. "If you come a bit closer, I'll pin up your braid. It's coming undone."

Lottie edged closer to Weza, and she skillfully replaced the hairpins Mama had put in Lottie's hair many hours ago. "There, that's better," Weza said.

"Thank you," said Lottie, still struggling to regain her composure.

"Think nothing of it," said Weza. The tall woman tied in front of Lottie had turned in their direction. The woman was so thin that she seemed nothing but sharp angles. Weza spoke for them both. "I'm Weza. And this is Lottie."

"Ruby," the woman said sullenly. "Your talking is going to get us in trouble."

Slye interrupted their conversation with a crack of his whip. "Everybody up. If you all got energy enough to talk, you got energy enough to walk."

Ruby gave Weza an I-told-you-so look as the women got up. Slye snapped his whip several inches from Weza's face. She squared her broad shoulders and never flinched, and to Lottie's surprise, Slye turned away.

The hours passed slowly. Lottie saw the dog star rise on the blue horizon as daylight faded. It grew colder. The chill from the frozen ground gradually crept up Lottie's legs until she shivered with every step. She thought of Mama as she slogged onward, clutching her tow bag to her heart. Mama wearing her gray dress and red-checkered apron in the warm, white-washed Williamsburg kitchen, full of the yeasty smell of just-baked bread. Mama's face, lighting up as it always did whenever she saw Lottie. Mama's arms encircling her. Lottie said softly to herself, "Mama, oh Mama, when will I see you again?"

In the gray twilight, the coffle neared the outskirts of a village and slowed its pace. They came to a dingy brick building with iron bars on the windows. Lottie guessed this must be a slave pen. She had heard of them, but she had never seen one. Slye banged on the door, and a few minutes later, a stooped, toothless man, holding an oil lamp, opened the door.

"Oh, it's you," he said to Slye.

"Got room for these?" Slye indicated the slaves.

"You can have the place to yourself tonight. I'll get the keys."

The pen had two cells. The women were put in one; the men in the other. Lottie was relieved to have the rope halter taken off, and she rubbed her sore neck as she slumped down in the straw strewn on the floor. There was no heat, and Slye, Ferris, and the custodian disappeared with the lamp once the women were in the cell.

"Come over here, Lottie," Weza said with such kindness in her voice that Lottie found it irresistible. "Stay next to me. Come close. It'll be warmer."

Lottie gratefully moved nearer to the older woman. Ruby and another woman were talking quietly. Weza loosened her outer shawl and put it and her arm around Lottie's shoulders. Lottie began to cry quietly and then losing all control, she cried in the hopeless and heartbroken way she had seen people weep at burials. For her, separation from Mama was a kind of death.

"There, there," Weza said. "Get it all out." After a few minutes, Weza began singing in a hushed voice that grew

Slave pen in Alexandria, Virginia

Library of Congress,
Prints and Photographs Division
[LC-B8171-2297]

stronger as she progressed. Her rich voice conveyed the sorrow the slaves all felt. Gradually, the others joined in:

Sometimes I feel like a motherless child,
Sometimes I feel like a motherless child,
A long way from home.

In the jail office, Slye and Ferris sat around a crude table with the warden, sharing a drink from Slye's flask.

"Give me the whip," Ferris said. "I'll shut up that yelping."

Slye fingered the whip that never was far from his hand. "Leave them alone," he said.

"First it's singing, then it will be running off," Ferris protested.

"Stow it," Slye said. "That's how they pray. Haven't you ever been by one of their churches and heard their music?"

Ferris laughed. "Since when do you care anything about praying?"

"I like the singing. Do you have a problem with that?" Slye scowled at Ferris, and grasped the whip handle in a threatening gesture. Ferris let it drop.

"What news of the war?" Slye asked the jailor, taking another pull from the flask before passing it to the others.

"I've heard there are Federal soldiers east and south of here," the jailor said. "And old Mrs. Streetman claimed they robbed her smokehouse, down by Old Town Creek. There must be an awful lot of those bluecoats, because people say they see them everywhere. Every time something disappears they blame the Yankees when as likely as not, it's somebody local causing the problem."

"There are lots of Yankees between here and Hampton," Slye said, still fingering his whip. "And they're bad for business. Nobody wants to buy slaves. Everybody wants to sell. I'm taking this lot south when I get a few more head." He took another drink and belched. "It's time to call it a night," he said, standing up to leave.

Chapter 3

Far from Home

For the next several days the coffle moved like a snake from village to village, plantation to plantation. At each stop, Slye purchased slaves. Lottie plodded along with the others, thinking of Mama and repeating to herself the promise she had made that last day. "I'll be strong. I'll survive," she said over and over.

One rainy night after a long, dreary day on the road, Slye and Ferris locked the slaves in an abandoned cow barn and disappeared. As they huddled together in the darkness, Lottie asked Weza, "Why does everybody seem to be selling slaves?"

"I'm making it my business to find out," said Weza. "You've probably noticed that every time I get a chance, I talk with the others. One of the men told me there are Union soldiers south of here and more coming all the time. He said the slave owners are afraid the Confederates won't be able to protect their land and property. So they're willing to sell their slaves cheap."

"It's all right with me," Lottie said. "Slye doesn't pay as much attention to us now with more slaves to keep in line. Weza, what's going to happen to us?"

"I don't know, child," Weza said. "Slye will steer clear of the Union troops in the area, and everyone thinks he'll soon put us on a boat to Norfolk or Portsmouth. Once we're across Hampton Roads, they'll march us south to the Carolina cotton fields."

"Back home, I heard that Yankees have tails," Lottie said, burrowing into the sweet-smelling hay for warmth. "And that they hitch slaves up to wagons."

"Nonsense," said Weza, reassuringly. "I've never seen anyone, anywhere with a tail. And as for slaves pulling wagons, they don't need us for that kind of work. They've got plenty of mules and horses."

Lottie turned over in her mind what Weza had said. "I don't understand what this war is all about," Lottie said after a while.

"When Mr. Lincoln became president, the Southern states formed their own government, the Confederacy. The Northern states went to war in order to bring the Southern states back into the Union."

"Why didn't the Southerners like President Lincoln?"

"They didn't like his views on slavery."

"I heard some people say he's going to free us," Lottie said.

"I've heard that too, but I don't know if he can do that. I do know when people run off to the Yankees, they don't get sent back to their masters." Weza eased off her worn shoes and made herself comfortable in the hay.

"Maybe the stories about Lincoln freeing the slaves are true. All the stories I heard about slaves traders are true," said Lottie.

"That Slye and Ferris look like they escaped from the bottomless pit," Weza said. "Yet so far we've been getting fed, and we've always had someplace dry to sleep."

"In barns and sheds," Lottie said bitterly. "We're treated like animals. I hate them. They only keep us alive because they paid money for us."

"It does no good to hate," Weza said, taking handfuls of hay and spreading it over Lottie's legs. "It takes too much out of you. We'll need all the strength we have. Right now, we better sleep, if we can."

That night, Lottie dreamed about Mama. It was a dream she had before. In it Mama was running from men with baying dogs. Then Mama stumbled, and the dogs leapt on her, yelping. They shredded her dress and tore the flesh from her leg. "No, no, stop!" Lottie screamed and came fully awake.

Weza reached out to comfort Lottie, putting a cool hand on her forehead. "What's the matter, child?" she asked.

"Mama was attacked by dogs," Lottie said.

"It was only a dream," said Weza.

"It really happened to her when she was my age. Dogs chewed her leg. Now she limps."

"This time, it was only a dream," Weza said, trying to reassure Lottie. "Your mama is all right."

"Weza, I'm scared."

"I know, child. We're all scared. Try to get some sleep now. It will be morning soon enough."

Lottie slept fitfully. When the gray light of early morning filtered through chinks in the barn, she got up feeling tired. Soon the coffle was out on the road again.

It snowed that morning. The slaves struggled on. Lottie had always thought snow was pretty. Now it made her wet and cold. She wondered how many birds and other woodland creatures would die from the cold during the coming night.

Snow was gradually transforming the gray landscape, shrouding trees and fields. Wind drove snow into Lottie's face, and she looked down as she tramped on. Weza had helped her stow her tow bag inside her coat lining, and from time to time she felt with her hand to make sure it was still secure. Occasionally, she checked Slye's whereabouts. She did not want to be caught by a surprise blow from his whip. But even he seemed subdued by the snow, and he rode along with his collar turned up and his hat jammed down to his eyes, still holding the whip.

Without warning, Lottie slipped on a patch of ice, hidden by the snow. She fell to her knees, the halter rope burned her and jerked the other women as she fell. As she tried to get up, Lottie saw Slye coming. His whip fell across her back, and she collapsed into the snow, waiting for the next blow.

Slye raised his whip, and Weza stepped between him and Lottie. Weza reached down and pulled Lottie to her feet. Weza brushed off the snow with a purposeful movement and sheltered Lottie, turning her broad back to Slye.

Slye lowered his whip and gave a signal to Ferris who prodded the lead man. The coffle lurched forward again. Lottie's back burned where the whip had stung through her coat. Her legs felt shaky, but she went forward with the others.

"Thank you," Lottie said to Weza when they stopped to rest. The slaves huddled on the falling-down porch of an abandoned slave cabin. It was cold, but under the porch roof the warped floorboards were dry. "Slye scares me," Lottie confided to Weza. "I feel like he is always watching, just waiting for me to step out of line."

Weza gave Lottie a reassuring pat. "Try not to worry about him," she said. "He gives us all that feeling."

They were silent for a few minutes, then Ruby leaned toward them. She pointed to Weza's earrings and asked, "Where did you get those gold earbobs?"

Weza was glad for a change of subject. "They were given to me nearly forty years ago by a freedman named Otis," she said. "He was working to buy my freedom when he was killed in a sawmill accident."

"They sure are pretty," Ruby said.

"I've never met a slave woman who didn't think so," said Weza, reaching up to touch them. "Inside there are words. I can't read, but one says, 'Take these,' and the other says, 'and my heart.' Have a look, Lottie," she said, lowering her head.

"I can't read either," Lottie said, studying the gold loops. "And I can't make out a thing."

"Let me look," Ruby said. Weza bent her head toward the tall woman. "I can see writing on the inside," she said. "It's awfully small."

They stopped talking as Ferris approached carrying a bucket of water, a dipper, and a gunny sack. They drank the icy water, and he took gray bread from the sack, giving each of them a small, hard piece.

A few minutes later they were back on the road. The snow turned to sleet. Ice clung to barren tree branches, and the deep ruts in the road froze, making the walking more difficult. The slaves in front of Lottie broke up the ice, and she felt like she was stepping on broken glass. A slave without shoes, ahead of Lottie, must have cut his foot because he left bloody footprints, like poppies in the snow. Lottie looked down thankfully at her mud-encrusted shoes and kept moving with the others.

They traveled for several hours with woods on both sides of the road. Finally, they came to an open field filled with swirling snow. Slye raised his hand, giving the signal for them to halt. Before them they saw a bloated horse. It had been dead for several days. Next to the horse were several bodies, only half-covered with newly spaded earth. A shattered wagon lay on its side amid some broken crates and other debris.

The rope around Lottie's neck suddenly pulled tight. She turned to see Weza stooping to pick up something. Lottie anxiously looked at Slye, wondering if he'd seen Weza, but his attention was fixed on the abandoned battlefield.

"Yankees. That settles it," Lottie heard Slye say to Ferris. "We're heading toward the river, tomorrow. It's time we got this lot out of the area. The bluebellies look like they got trounced here, but they're getting too close for comfort."

Chapter 4
Neither Good nor Bad

After a long, tiring journey by train and wagon with her new owner's overseer, Clara Shadwell, Lottie's mother, finally arrived at Emma Howell's big, white house. It was on the outskirts of Winchester and stood on a hill overlooking a valley. The overseer took her to Mrs. Howell immediately.

Mrs. Howell was a middle-aged, thin, blond woman who once must have been pretty, but now there was a network of fine lines around her eyes and mouth. She was sitting in the parlor dressed in an elegant riding costume and had obviously just returned from an outing. "You must be Clara," she said, as if annoyed with having to bother with her new slave. "You'll need your instructions. We have thirty-eight of our people here. But you're not to feed them. I don't want to catch you giving slaves food from my table." She paused and looked down her angular nose at Clara. "Mr. Howell is important locally, very important. He supplies the best horses in the Shenandoah Valley to the generals in Richmond. I like to entertain, and I'm known for the table I set. You'll do my cooking and in addition, I want the kitchen kept spotless. Do you understand me?"

"Yes, 'um," said Clara, cowed by her new owner's brusque manner.

"Henrietta, my housekeeper, will show you around," said Mrs. Howell. "I'm sending the hopeless girl who has been trying to cook for me back to the fields. You can begin by preparing dinner tonight." She pulled an embroidered bell cord.

A moment later Henrietta appeared. She took Clara to the kitchen. Henrietta was a stocky, barrel-shaped woman who in spite of her size moved about with surprising ease. "Mrs. Howell hasn't had a good cook for a while," Henrietta said when they were alone. "So she hasn't entertained. I'm afraid you're in for it. She's planning dinner parties and even a ball." As tired and as dispirited as Clara felt, she took off her coat and put on an apron she found on a peg.

"What's Mr. Howell like?" Clara asked.

"He's not like she is," said Henrietta, rolling her eyes. "But don't worry, you'll be all right here."

"I always told my little girl, Lottie...," Clara paused for a moment. Saying Lottie's name out loud brought a flood of wrenching memories. She continued solemnly, "...most places are neither good nor bad, just ordinary. I'm glad they don't mistreat us."

Two weeks later, Henrietta approached Clara in the kitchen, a rectangular, brick building in back of the main house. It was a place where Henrietta could talk without fear of being overheard. The kitchen had a huge fireplace facing the door with baking ovens beside it. Copper pans hung from hooks near the fireplace. Clara had to keep these pots shining, and when Henrietta came in, Clara was bending over a basin, scouring a pan. Henrietta pulled up a chair and seated herself next to Clara.

"As soon as you came here, I took a liking to you," said Henrietta. "I knew you'd cause no trouble. But I'm concerned about you. Won't you tell me what's ailing you, Clara?"

"Nothing," Clara replied, scrubbing harder on the pan she was scouring.

"You've lost weight since you've come here, and you're so sad," Henrietta said. "You haven't even met most of the other slaves. Why not join us Saturday afternoon? There's a baptism and a social down by the river."

"I'm not interested in meeting anyone," Clara replied. "And I needed to lose weight. I was too heavy in Williamsburg."

"Come on, Clara, you were as thin as a sheet of paper when you came here," Henrietta insisted. "What's bothering you?"

"I've already told you," Clara said.

"What do you mean?" Henrietta asked.

"I feel like someone ripped my heart out. Working for someone who sold away my only child nags at me all the time," Clara replied. "I can't forget. I don't want to forget. How can I be happy and go around as if nothing's wrong, when everything's wrong?"

"I told you about my babies and their father," Henrietta said. "I've lost two children. One with croup; the other with fever. And their father died of the same fever that took the baby."

"I know you've got your sorrows, too," said Clara. "But at least you know that your children are safe, that no one is hurting them, that they aren't suffering."

"I heard about a slave woman who drowned her own children so they wouldn't suffer under a hard master," said Henrietta. "Yet after losing two children, I know anything is better than death. You've got to have hope. Sometimes that's all there is."

"I do hope," Clara replied. "Whenever I hear the wind blowing or see the rain falling, I wonder if my child is out in the weather, and I hope with all my heart that she's warm and dry. I hope someone is being good to her. Yet, I fear just the opposite. Sometimes I think I failed bringing her up. Lottie's quiet and thoughtful, and she takes everything too much to heart."

"She's like her mother," said Henrietta.

"That's why it was hard for me to teach her to be any other way," said Clara. "Now I'm afraid she won't be able to deal with the harshness of her new life."

"You need to try to adjust to your life here," Henrietta said.

"It's easy for you to say that," Clara replied, finishing the last pot and drying her hands on a dish towel. "You don't have to work from sun up to sun down for somebody who separated you from all that's dear to you in the world. I do. Each day to me is like pouring salt on an open wound. On some days I'm so full of hate that I could spit into each dish I cook. On other days, I don't care about anything." She sighed and sat down at the table with Henrietta.

"When you came here, you told me that you'd find Lottie someday," Henrietta said. "Have you totally given up hope of seeing her again?"

"Henrietta, I'm a grown woman. I'm a slave. I hope to be reunited with Lottie again, of course. But I really don't believe I'll ever see her again...anymore than I'll ever see her father again."

"You can't just give up," Henrietta said. "You've got to go on living."

"Why should I go on? What does life hold for me, except work and more work?" Clara replied.

"You might have other children someday," Henrietta ventured.

"I don't want other children. I want Lottie. And what if I had another child? The day would come when that child would be taken from me, too. I've always tried to make the best of things, and what's it got me?"

Henrietta did not answer immediately. A few moments later she said, "I know what you say is true, but others keep hoping and keep going, in spite of everything."

"They're stronger than I am, or just more foolish," Clara replied.

Henrietta sighed. Talking with Clara was frustrating.

Chapter 5
Freedom Is Near

The coffle headed for the James River. The weather turned warmer, and the snow melted, leaving puddles in the road and soggy grass alongside it. Lottie could tell little difference in the countryside. They passed through scrubby pine woods, farm lands, and isolated villages. They avoided the main roads. Slye no longer was buying and selling slaves, and it seemed to Lottie that they progressed more rapidly now.

Late that afternoon as the light faded, Lottie thought she heard gunshots and turned to look at Weza. She had noticed the distant rifle reports, and she walked along with her head inclined toward the direction of the sound. Slye had heard the gunfire, too; and his whip fell on the men. "Pick up the pace!" he yelled.

The foot-weary slaves, fearing the lash, hurried along the road. Lottie's legs were shorter than the others' and she almost had to run to keep up. Finally, they came to a crossroads and took a narrower road. A half mile down the road, Slye called a halt, and Lottie, breathing heavily, sat down next to Weza.

Everyone was silent for a few minutes, listening for the sound of gunfire. Lottie whispered to Weza, "Was that fighting?"

"Most likely, considering the way Slye reacted."

Then Lottie heard the crack and snap of gunfire again. This time it was nearer, and the sound seemed to come from another direction although it was hard to tell since the road they had taken was winding. "What's going on?" she asked Weza.

"Slye's trying to avoid running into any Union soldiers. This part of the peninsula is full of them, and if there's one thing the Yankees hate, it's slave traders."

Suddenly they heard the telltale clopping of horses, traveling fast. Slye looked warily around. No regular travelers would be riding at such a pace. Something was amiss. "Get out of sight," he ordered, indicating a thick screen of underbrush on the side of the road. He cracked the whip. "Move it!" he yelled. "Get down, over there!"

The whip fell on the chained men who hustled to do as they were ordered. Lottie and the other women scrambled along after them. They crouched behind the bushes. Lottie clasped her hands around her knees, trying to stay still and balance herself at the same time. Ferris and Slye dismounted, and Slye led the horses into the woods. Ferris knelt down nearby, his gun ready.

Moments later, two blue-coated soldiers appeared on horseback. Lottie held her breath. The soldiers galloped by, never looking in the direction of the slaves. It seemed that they had been hiding for a very long time when Slye gave the order for the slaves to get up. "We'll stay off the road for a while," he said. His brow was furrowed, and Lottie thought he looked scared.

The slaves began to pick their way single file through the woods, following Slye. First came the chained men, then the women with Lottie and Weza bringing up the rear. Lottie kept her eyes on Ruby's narrow back as they made their way through the woods. The ground was uneven, and Lottie had learned that if she watched Ruby's movements, she could anticipate when the rope might burn her neck.

They traveled parallel to the road. Fallen trees, patches of thick undergrowth, and gullies caused by winter rains slowed them down. Slye and Ferris had to dismount and walk their horses. Lottie and Weza struggled on with the others for an hour or more as darkness gathered. Finally, they stopped to rest on the damp ground.

Weza leaned toward Lottie and whispered, "I'm going, as soon as it's dark enough." She showed Lottie where her rope was cut almost all the way through. Lottie squinted at the rope, trying in the dim light to see what Weza was showing her. "I've thought about it, and I just can't leave you here on your own." When no one was looking, Weza took a three-inch broken piece of a knife blade from her skirt hem and gave it to Lottie.

Lottie clamped her fingers around the cold blade, fearful that Slye or Ferris would look in her direction. This must be what Weza picked up near the battlefield.

"You've got to cut the rope as you walk," Weza whispered. "Make sure no one sees you. Just hold the rope like it's burning your neck and saw away little by little."

"I'm not sure I can do it," Lottie said, biting her lip. She was terrified Slye or Ferris would catch her with the knife, but she dreaded the idea of Weza leaving without her. How could she survive without Weza?

"This is our chance, maybe our only chance," Weza stopped talking as Slye looked in their direction.

"Where will we go? And what if they send dogs after us?" Lottie asked when Slye turned away and began talking with Ferris.

"We'll head toward that gunfire and take our chances."

Fear gripped Lottie. What would happen if Slye caught her? She could hardly stand when he got the slaves up again. He took a lantern from his saddlebag and lit it. He returned to the head of the line of slaves, leading the way. Ferris stationed himself near the end of the chained men and followed the glittering light from Slye's lantern.

Lottie kept watching Slye and Ferris. They seemed to be paying no particular attention to her as the darkness deepened. She swallowed the bile that rose in her throat, recalling that her mother had told her to be strong. She took a deep breath and put her hands on her neck rope. With one hand she held the rope, and with the other carefully moved the knife blade back and forth. Strand by strand, she cut the rope.

Fifteen minutes later she had almost cut through it. She turned to look at Weza. The older woman gestured with one hand. Lottie understood it was not yet time. She began worrying about Ruby. What would Ruby do when she realized Lottie and Weza were trying to escape? Weza had gotten to know the other slave women, but Ruby had never responded to Weza's friendliness. Lottie was afraid that Ruby would cry out as soon as they cut themselves free.

Lottie felt a slight tug on her rope. Weza nodded to Lottie, and with trembling fingers, she cut the slender piece of rope that still attached her to the other women. Feeling the tension on her rope slacken, Ruby turned and stared, but she said nothing. Taking the knife, Weza cut the strand of rope tying her to Lottie. A moment later, they plunged into the darkness.

Lottie's heart was pounding like a huge drum as she followed the dark shape in front of her. Weza held her breath as she made her way through the woods slowly and carefully, fearing a misstep would make a noise that would alert Slye or Ferris. Ever since she had found the broken knife, Weza had planned for this moment. Now as she led Lottie through the trees toward the road they had traveled earlier, Weza wondered if she was doing the right thing.

As soon as they were well away from the others, they began to run. They reached the road, and once there, Weza stopped for a moment, breathing heavily. She listened. No one seemed to be following. "This way," she said, hoping her voice didn't reveal her fear. "Come on." Side by side, Weza and Lottie hastened along the shadowy road.

Slye had been leading the slaves through the woods for almost an hour when he turned and signaled to Ferris. He joined Slye at the head of the coffle. "We're heading back to the road. I don't want to miss the turn to the farm where we'll spend the night," Slye said. "It's probably safe now."

Ten minutes later, they were out of the woods. Ferris suddenly shouted, "The little girl and the old woman are gone!"

"Dad blame a blue-eyed black snake!" Slye cursed. He rushed to the tall woman now at the end of the line. "How long have they been gone?" he screamed.

Ruby stood before him with her head lowered. She said nothing. Slye struck Ruby on the back with his whip, again, and again. She winced from the searing pain, wavering from the force of the blows. But she continued to stare impassively at the ground.

"You people can't be trusted; you're as thick as thieves," Slye said, shaking his whip at the others, as he strode away.

Ruby's back burned, and she warily raised her head once she was certain Slye was no longer near. She put her hand into her skirt pocket. Her fingers found Weza's gold earrings. She fondled them lovingly, hoping she could find someone soon to pierce her ears.

"What do we do now?" Ferris asked Slye as he resumed his place at the head of the coffle.

"Not much we can do until morning," Slye said, kicking a clod of dirt by the side of the road. "I can't believe those two got away. We'll get some dogs. Go after them as soon as it's light. I'll teach them a thing or two. Right now we need to get the rest hunkered down for the night."

Chapter 6
Like a Bird in the Sky

Lottie and Weza kept to the road until they came to the fork where they had turned off earlier. "We'll go back the way we came," said Weza. "It's dangerous for us to be out on the road this time of night. We need a place to rest until later."

"Where?" Lottie asked.

"We went over a bridge earlier," said Weza. "The water's high from all the rain and snow, but there's still a grassy bank under the arch. We'll stay there until we're sure everybody's asleep."

They met no one on the road. It was suppertime, and they passed farms with yellow squares of light coming from kitchens and dining rooms. A dog barked, but no one came to investigate. It wasn't long before they came to the bridge.

Lottie and Weza made their way down the bank. "We'll collect some leaves, have a drink of water, and rest," Weza said, busying herself gathering leaves. A few minutes later, they were settled under the bridge. "Try to sleep," said Weza. "I'll wake you in a couple of hours." Lottie leaned against Weza, listening to the chattering water. She was bone tired and in a few minutes fell asleep. Weza stayed awake, worrying.

Chapter 6

It was pitch-black when Weza woke Lottie. "Time to go," she said.

Lottie stirred from the leaf nest. She felt stiff from sleeping sitting up. She was hungry, but she didn't say anything. She knew they had no food.

Weza was uncertain which way to go. She wasn't sure how to find the Yankees, and she wanted to get as far away as possible from the slave traders. She wondered how long they had before sunup. They couldn't travel the roads during the day because they didn't have slave passes. If anyone stopped them, they would be sent back to Slye.

Weza chose the most likely direction and started forward with determination. They walked for a long time. A half-moon rose above the trees and silvered the road ahead. It seemed to Lottie that they'd been on the road the whole night. She kept looking behind her, wondering when they would be caught. A twig snapped somewhere and she jumped.

After a while the moon set, and the sky began to lighten in front of them. "We have to find a place to hide during the day," Weza said. "We can't risk someone asking for our passes."

As morning spread over the sky, Lottie noticed for the first time that Weza wasn't wearing her earrings. "What happened to your earrings?" Lottie asked.

"I gave them to Ruby so she wouldn't tell on us," said Weza, absently feeling her empty earlobes.

"How could you give them up?"

"Losing them is a small price to pay for freedom," Weza said, her voice quavering.

"But your memories...," protested Lottie.

"I'll remember Otis to my dying day, with or without the earrings. I wrestled with what to do about Ruby, and then suddenly I knew. It was as if I'd kept the earrings all these years for one purpose. Otis would approve. How long do you think a woman my age would last in the cotton fields?"

"I'm sorry, Weza," Lottie said.

"Don't fret about it, child," Weza said. "We've got other things to worry about. Let's look at that old shed." She pointed to a falling-down tobacco shed, half hidden by trees. "Maybe we can hide there." They left the road to investigate.

As they neared the shed, they heard dogs, far in the distance, the yelping of hounds following a scent. Lottie panicked. She didn't have to ask Weza what the sound meant. She knew dogs were on their trail. What would happen to them if they were caught?

"We'll keep going," Weza said. She put a reassuring hand on Lottie's shoulder. "I think we should go this way now." She pointed to a field, filled with dry corn stalks left from last fall's harvest.

Lottie and Weza hurried across the field. Weza didn't know where they were going. She just wanted to get away from the baying dogs. They crossed an orchard and came to a raging, winter-swollen stream. The sun was fully up now. High wispy clouds drifted in the blue sky overhead.

"Let's walk in the water. Maybe we can delay the dogs. They can't follow our scent in the water," Weza said, hiking up her skirts and stepping boldly into the rapidly coursing stream.

Lottie followed her example. The brisk water stung her feet as she plunged in after Weza.

They hadn't gone far when the stream bed narrowed, and the water grew deeper. It was nearly up to Lottie's knees when Weza took her hand. They climbed out of the water and up the steep bank.

Lottie's shoes squished as she hurried along beside Weza. The bottom of Lottie's dress had gotten wet, and she was shaking with cold. She kept thinking of Mama, and the dogs tearing her leg. Memories and dreams heightened the terror that had gripped Lottie at the first sound of the dogs.

The yowling and yapping grew louder. Weza and Lottie started to run. They stumbled down a hill toward the shelter of a clump of leafless trees.

Suddenly, rising silently up in front of them over the tops of the trees, they saw a huge red-and-blue, round thing, as big as a house. It cleared the trees and drifted dreamlike in their direction. Startled, Weza and Lottie stopped and stood gaping at the thing. A basket hung from the huge ball, decorated with American flags. Two tiny men were in the basket. Two long lines trailed from it to the ground.

"What is it!" Lottie asked in horror. "What is it?"

"I don't know," Weza said. She swallowed hard, trying to get rid of the great lump of fear that had risen in her throat. "I've never seen anything like it. God help us! Come on, into the woods!"

**A drawing of John LaMountain's balloon
ascension at Fortress Monroe, 1861**

Leslie's *Illustrated Weekly*, 1861;
Courtesy of the Casemate Museum, Fort Monroe

In the observation balloon, a soldier studied Lottie and
Weza through his telescope. At first he thought they were just
frightened by the balloon. It was a common reaction. Then he
heard the dogs. He had heard them earlier, but since he was
studying enemy troop movements in the other direction, he
had paid no attention to their insistent yelping. He turned toward the sound and scanned the area, spotting the dogs and
two men on horses, one carrying a bullwhip.

"Look over there," the soldier said, passing the telescope
to the telegrapher, who had been inspecting the hairlike telegraph wires wrapped in blue silk.

The telegrapher quickly understood what was going on. "Slavers, after a child and an old woman," he said. "I'm going to telegraph the ground."

"Hurry up!" the soldier said. "There isn't much time."

The telegrapher thought about what he should say as he surveyed the countryside again with the telescope. He must choose his words carefully. He easily found Weza's red kerchief, and he watched the old woman and the girl frantically running through the leafless woods. The frenzied dogs were less than a mile away. He noted the roads, the stream, and the ravine.

He tapped out the message: "Dogs and slavers gaining on little girl and grandmother. Need assistance immediately." He consulted his map for a few seconds. His finger flew on the telegraph key as he gave precise information on their location. When he was done, he hastily added, "For God's sake, somebody help them."

Chapter 7
Contraband of War

The howling and yelping were growing closer. Lottie and Weza raced down a hillside into a ravine, half slipping, half sliding. Lottie feared at any minute the dogs would break out of the woods. She looked behind her, expecting to see them charging toward her. She failed to see the fallen branch in her path. She twisted her ankle and fell. Weza grabbed her and pulled her to her feet, thrusting her toward the hill on the other side of the ravine.

They were gasping for breath as they clambered up the hill. At its top, they paused for a moment to look behind them. Brown and white spotted dogs, yelping furiously with their noses to the ground, bounded out of the woods on the other side of the ravine. The men were out of sight. The dogs would attack before the men could call them off.

"Come on," Weza said, looking about her as she ran. She saw a thicket not far off. She dove into the thick tangle of brambles and bushes, pulling Lottie in behind her.

Weza fell to her knees and edged her way along the ground. Lottie did the same. Branches stung their faces. Brambles tore skin and clothing. Finally, Weza stopped and pulled Lottie close.

The yelping grew nearer. Soon it was replaced by growling and barking as the dogs surrounded the thicket. One dog began crawling toward them, baring his long teeth and snarling. Lottie buried her head in Weza's chest, waiting for the dog to reach them. Lottie's heart beat fast. She heard a horse neigh somewhere nearby. She raised her head. The dog lunged toward her neck. Weza's arm flashed out to protect Lottie. The dog's teeth sunk into Weza's sleeve. She shook the dog loose. He snarled and snapped, sinking his teeth again into her sleeve.

Four horsemen came into view. "Fire in the air," one commanded. Lottie heard a series of loud shots, and the pack of dogs surrounding them fled, all except the one holding on to Weza's sleeve. Lottie saw snatches of blue uniforms through the tangle of undergrowth.

"Corporal, see to that dog!" a man commanded. "And stay with the woman and girl." One of the soldiers dismounted. Forcing his way through the briars, he struck the dog with his rifle butt. The dog let go of Weza's sleeve with a yelp and ran off after the others.

The corporal leaned down. "You can come out," he said. "You'll be safe now."

Lottie and Weza carefully picked their way out of the brambles. Lottie looked at Weza. Her kerchief was askew, and there were leaves and sticks in her hair. There was an ugly red welt across her face, and her dress was muddy. Lottie put her hand up to touch her own hair and felt the debris caught in her braids.

The corporal offered them his canteen. He was a muscular young man with side whiskers and a bushy mustache. Now that the danger had passed, he seemed ill at ease. "Are you all right?" he asked.

"A few scrapes, that's all," Weza said, gratefully taking a drink of water after Lottie had finished. "We'll be good as new in a few days." She passed the canteen back to the corporal and began straightening her scarf and tidying her hair.

They heard gunfire, and before long the other soldiers returned. They dismounted and joined the corporal. One of the soldiers, somewhat older than the others, tipped his hat and spoke to Weza. "We've chased off the slavers for you, ma'am," he said. She looked questioningly into the man's ruddy face, half-hidden under a brown beard. In her sixty years no white man had ever tipped his hat to her. She saw that he was sincere, and she nodded her head slightly in response as she had seen white women do.

Lottie's attention was riveted on a broad-chested soldier, holding a whip, a whip just like Slye's. He flicked it in the air, and it made a snapping sound. Lottie backed away.

The soldier, noticing her retreat, coiled the whip and put it in his saddlebag. "Don't be scared," he said. "I picked up this to show the folks back in Maine. We wounded one of the slavers, and he dropped it."

"Sergeant," the corporal asked the man who had spoken to Weza, "what will we do with them? We can't just let them go."

"Look at that little girl," the sergeant said, pointing to Lottie. "She's nothing but a bone with some skin stretched over it. Now I believe what the abolitionists are always going on about. We'll take them with us. They're contraband of war."

Lottie glanced down at her skeletal wrists and hands. They looked like the leafless trees all around them. Weza took a deep breath and asked, "Will you please tell me what 'contraband of war' means?"

"Ma'am," the sergeant said, "simply put, it means that you're confiscated enemy property. You're free while you're under the protection of the United States government. We'll take you back to our camp for the time being. Are you able to walk? It's not far."

Fighting her weariness, Weza stood a little bit taller. "I'd be proud to walk into freedom," she said, "but this child is wore out."

The sergeant turned to the corporal. "Better put her up behind you."

The corporal swung up into his saddle and with a quick movement swept Lottie up behind him as easily as if she were a doll. Lottie reached inside her coat, reassuring herself that she had not lost her tow bag in all the excitement.

Twenty minutes later, they came to an imposing brick house with many chimneys. Behind the house were horses, tents, and soldiers. Above the field to the left of the house, many feet in the air, they saw the huge ball with the basket hanging beneath it.

**Sketch of an observation balloon in
a Union camp near the James River**

Courtesy of the Casemate Museum, Fort Monroe

Weza turned to the sergeant. "What's that?" she asked. "It sure scared us."

"A reconnaissance balloon," he replied. "We use balloons to keep track of enemy troops. The soldiers up there saw you two instead of Johnny Reb this morning. They asked us to help you out. You were lucky. We were mounted up and just about to leave camp to go on patrol."

Weza and Lottie waved at the men in the balloon. The man who had watched the rescue through his telescope waved back. The telegrapher raised his arms in triumph.

The soldiers took Lottie and Weza to one of the many outbuildings that surrounded the great house. A young woman met them at the door. "Come in," she said with a friendly smile. "I'm Ida, and I take care of escaped slaves that come into camp. You look pretty tuckered." Smells of coffee, bacon sizzling in a pan, and fresh-baked spoonbread greeted Lottie and Weza as they entered the cabin. "Sit in front of the fire. I'll bring you some food," said Ida, indicating the bench by the fireplace. "Later you can tell me all about how you got here."

After they had eaten and told their story, Lottie and Weza lay side by side on a pallet in the loft of the one-room cabin. Lottie touched Weza's hand to see if she was awake. "What's going to happen to us?" Lottie asked.

"I don't know, child," Weza said, giving Lottie's hand a slight squeeze. "But we're not going to be sent back. We're not slaves anymore." Reassured, Lottie shut her eyes and fell into an exhausted sleep.

Chapter 8

Lung Fever

The days passed slowly for Lottie's mother. One sunny day, Henrietta came into the kitchen, where Clara was kneading bread dough. "Can you believe this weather?" Henrietta asked. "It feels like spring, even though it's still February. Let's go outside. We'll take a walk. Since the missus is going out for dinner tonight, you have no excuse."

Clara smiled. "You've talked me into it. I do enjoy a warm day in winter," she said. "I'll finish up here and get my coat."

By the time they returned, Henrietta was hopeful that Clara might adjust to her new life. "That wasn't so bad, was it?" Henrietta asked.

"It was good to get out," said Clara. "I had no idea this place was so big. I especially liked seeing the foal. He was all legs." Her face clouded. "Lottie would have loved him."

That night the temperature dropped to freezing, and two inches of snow fell by morning. Clara woke with chills. Mrs. Howell was planning a dinner party that evening, and Clara got up feeling sick all over. She went to the kitchen to take charge of the preparations. Her head ached as she made a wine sauce and set beef to marinate in it. She felt more and more feverish as the day wore on. Yet she baked paper-thin cookies, decorating them with nuts and frosting and shelled pecans for two pecan pies. She felt weak and dizzy as she cut potatoes for a sweet potato casserole.

Everyone was so busy getting ready for the dinner that no one paid attention to Clara. No one, except Henrietta. The housekeeper noticed Clara's weary movements and the slight stoop of her shoulders as she went about her tasks. "You should be in bed," Henrietta said. "I've already told the missus that you're sick."

"What did she say?" asked Clara, knowing that her mistress only thought about herself.

"You know how she is," said Henrietta. "She said it was all right for you to be sick after the dinner's over."

"I'll do just that," Clara replied. She put the casserole into the oven and sat down for a moment. "Mrs. Howell will make my life miserable if I don't cook for her party."

Henrietta went into the dining room and set the table with the best white linen tablecloth and the flower-patterned Wedgwood dinnerware. She was just taking out the fragile glassware from the mahogany china cabinet when Lucy, one of the parlormaids, found her. She was a simple-minded, hardworking girl of sixteen. "Clara's real sick," Lucy said. "She asked me to fetch you." Henrietta put down the glass she was holding and rushed to the kitchen.

Clara sat at the kitchen worktable with her head on her arms. When Henrietta approached, Clara raised her head slightly. Henrietta put a hand on Clara's forehead. She was hot with fever. "You should be in bed," Henrietta said. "Lucy, help me get her to the quarters."

With Lucy's help, Henrietta got Clara to her cramped, dark room in the slave quarters. Henrietta put Clara in bed. "I'm cold," Clara said with a shiver.

The room was cold. Henrietta covered Clara with quilts, but her shivering did not stop. "Make a fire in the fireplace," Henrietta told Lucy. "And stay here 'til I get back. I need to see the missus."

"She's not going to like it if Clara spoils her dinner party," Lucy said.

"She'll have to postpone it or get in another cook from someplace else," Henrietta said. "Clara's too sick to cook."

Mrs. Howell was arranging a winter bouquet of holly for the dinner party when Henrietta brought her the news. "That Clara," Mrs. Howell said, pursing her mouth, "I can't risk ruining my party; I'll have to cancel. That Clara's a bother. She's sour all the time. She never smiles. Are you sure she isn't making it up?"

"She's pretty sick, ma'am," Henrietta said. "She can hardly stand up. She's as weak as a newborn calf."

"See that she's taken care of," Mrs. Howell said absentmindedly. "It's bad enough that she's sick. It would be worse if she dies. And bring me my pen and some paper. Have Jasper here in an hour to deliver my regrets." Jasper was the Howell's stableman. He was an old man with a bald head surrounded by a fringe of white hair. He was half-crippled from falling under a hay wagon when he was young. Mrs.

Howell frequently sent him on errands, since there was no danger of him running away.

"Clara's no better," Henrietta reported to Mrs. Howell the following day.

"Visit that slave woman, the one in town who knows herbs," Mrs. Howell said. "I'll write you a pass." She went to her desk and jotted a few words on a slip of paper. She took a small coin from her purse. "Give this to the woman for her trouble."

Later that evening after she had gotten the herbs, Henrietta boiled the dried leaves to make a drink for Clara. "Here, drink some of this," she said, putting her arm under Clara's head and holding her up so that she could take a sip. "This will bring your fever down."

"I can't swallow," Clara said hoarsely, slipping back onto the pillow.

"Please try," Henrietta insisted. She raised Clara's head again.

Clara managed to swallow a few teaspoons of hot liquid before she began to cough and choke.

That night and the following day Henrietta stayed by Clara's side, neglecting her usual duties. She was afraid Mrs. Howell would punish her, but she couldn't leave Clara.

That evening Mrs. Howell came into the quarters. She took one look at Clara. "Why didn't you tell me Clara was so sick?" Mrs. Howell complained. "Send Jasper for the herb woman."

The thin, bent herb woman came an hour later and examined Clara. "The grippe has gone into lung fever," she told Henrietta. "I'm not sure she'll pull through. The crisis hasn't come yet. And when it does, if she doesn't go then, she stands a chance."

"What can we do?" Henrietta asked.

"Somebody should stay with her," the herb woman said. "Keep her sponged down and comfortable. There's nothing else anybody can do."

"I'll stay with her," Henrietta said, drawing up a chair beside Clara's bed. Henrietta had never seen anyone so sick survive such a terrible fever.

Sometime later that night Lucy came in. "You go on. Get some sleep," she said. "The missus told me I should look out for a while."

Henrietta felt exhausted, but she didn't trust Lucy to stay awake. "I'm all right," she said. She got a damp cloth and placed it on Clara's feverish brow. The hours passed slowly. Finally, during the darkest hours of the night, Henrietta guessed that the crisis was near. Clara became delirious and kept calling, "Lottie? Lottie, where are you?"

As Clara pitifully called out again and again for Lottie, Henrietta didn't know what to do. She thought Clara was going to die.

"Lottie!" Clara called. "Where's Lottie?"

In desperation, Henrietta answered Clara, "Lottie's outside, Clara. You've got to get better or you can't see her. You're too sick for her to come in."

Clara didn't seem to understand. A few minutes later, she called out again. "Lottie?"

Henrietta repeated the simple formula. "She's outside. She can't come in until you're better." This time Clara seemed to understand. She breathed deeply and relaxed. But later that night, Clara's breathing grew irregular. She struggled for each breath. Henrietta worried that her breathing would stop altogether. But it didn't.

As dawn crept into the quarters, Clara's breathing grew easier and she fell into a deep sleep. Henrietta felt her forehead. The fever was down. The crisis had passed.

Later that day when Clara woke, she was weak. Henrietta brought her steaming broth in a blue-and-white porcelain dish with a long spout. It looked like a flattened-out, covered cream pitcher. Clara recognized it as an invalid feeder. "How are you?" Henrietta asked, sitting on the bed beside her friend.

"I dreamed Lottie was here," Clara said, her voice raspy. "She was in the next room. It was wonderful."

Henrietta had been worrying about the little lie she had told Clara. Now Henrietta smiled. She was convinced that she had done the right thing. "Here," she said, holding the invalid feeder to Clara's lips. "Try to drink a little broth."

Henrietta went back to her regular duties the following day, checking often on Clara. "You've survived the crisis," Henrietta told Clara cheerfully.

Clara smiled wanly at her friend. "Each day you'll grow stronger," Henrietta said, hoping what she said would be true.

Chapter 9
Grand Contraband Camp

Contrabands coming into Fortress Monroe

Drawing from a photograph by Adrian-Probasco,
courtesy of the Casemate Museum, Fort Monroe

Five days later, an escort of soldiers took Lottie and
Weza along with a convoy of supply wagons to Fortress
Monroe. Ida had told them they would be going to what
the slaves called Fortress Freedom. And so Lottie was surprised when they did not go inside the thick, gray stone
walls.

"I'm to take you to Grand Contraband Camp," a pink-cheeked, young soldier told them. "It's where all the contrabands live. You'll be living there, too."

Lottie and Weza accompanied the soldier into the sprawling village of shanties that made up the camp. The shanties were built of whatever was at hand: old packing cases, parts of broken wagons, barrels, burlap, and what appeared to be cast-off army tents.

Grand Contraband Camp built on the ruins of Hampton, Virginia

Harper's Weekly, June 14, 1862;
courtesy of the Casemate Museum, Fort Monroe

The young soldier took them to a square, wooden building. The upper part of the building had been burned, and the bottom half looked like it had once been a store. "Mrs. Prue looks after contrabands," he said. "She represents the American Missionary Association. It's a group that has come here to help escaped slaves. She'll take care of you. Just knock, and then go on in."

Mrs. Prue, a stout, middle-aged woman, dressed in black, was seated at a desk. She stood when Lottie and Weza came in the door. "Hello," she said, "I'm Mrs. Prue and my job is to help you get settled. Please be seated." She indicated two straight-backed chairs.

"What are your names?" Mrs. Prue asked, sitting down at her desk.

"I'm Louisa Adams," said Weza. "And this is Lottie Shadwell."

Mrs. Prue wrote their names in a ledger. "Before we begin, do you have any questions?" she asked.

In her life as a slave, Weza could not recall anyone white inviting her to ask a question. "I don't quite know what to ask," she said, momentarily taken aback. "But I would like to know what's going on here with all the soldiers?"

"Fortress Monroe remained in Federal hands when the war began," Mrs. Prue said, hoping she understood the sense of Weza's question. "Because we are deep in Confederate territory, the Union army is using the fortress as a staging area. They are massing troops here to retake the Virginia Peninsula and attack the Confederate capital at Richmond. The soldiers who brought you here are part of that campaign."

"Will we be safe here?" Weza asked.

Mrs. Prue laughed bitterly. "You'd think with all the soldiers around that former slaves would be safe," she said. "But we've had a few cases of former slaves being kidnaped and sold back into slavery in Rebel-held territory. The problem is that there are so many people coming and going in Grand Contraband Camp that it is hard to keep track of everyone. The army has more to do than worry about freed slaves."

"We'll be on our guard," Weza said resolutely.

"I don't mean to frighten you," said Mrs. Prue. "The chances of being kidnaped are remote. Your biggest problem here, I'm afraid, is overcrowding. In fact, I'm not sure where I'll put you."

"We aren't fussy," Weza said.

Mrs. Prue consulted a list on her desk. "The only place we have right now is a barn," she said, looking again at the list and shaking her head.

"That won't be a problem," said Weza. "We've been staying in barns and slave pens."

"Then it's settled," said Mrs. Prue, writing something on a list. "Now we need to see about clothes. Do you have anything other than what you're wearing?"

"No, ma'am," said Weza. "Just what you see."

Mrs. Prue looked them over for a moment. Her manner was brusque and businesslike, and Lottie felt self-conscious under her scrutiny. Weza had washed Lottie's tattered dress, but her coat was still mud-splattered from their ordeal in the woods. Her shoes were nearly ruined from the rough, wet roads. "I'll be right back," said Mrs. Prue, disappearing into another room.

Mrs. Prue came back with her arms full. "Most of the people who arrive here are completely destitute," she said.

"Some run away with only the clothes on their backs and don't even have shoes or a coat." She gave them each a gray wool blanket. "The blanket is from the Missionary Association and the clothes come from the Freedman's Relief Society. I'm not sure about the sizes." She handed them each a shift, a dress, and shoes and stockings. "If they don't fit, just bring them back and I'll give you others."

Lottie looked down at the brown, woolen dress the woman had given her. "Thank you," she managed to say, thinking it was the ugliest thing she had ever seen.

"Why this is very nice," Weza said graciously. "Our clothes are a mess, and neither of us have a blanket."

Mrs. Prue handed them each a soldier's mess kit. "This is from the United States government," she said. "And this comes from the Missionary Ladies Auxiliary in Boston. You'll find some personal items inside." She gave them little hand-sewn bags.

"We thank you," said Weza, speaking for them both.

Mrs. Prue rapidly wrote a couple of notations in a book on her desk. "If you come with me, I'll take you to your quarters."

Weza and Lottie followed Mrs. Prue outside and walked with her through Grand Contraband Camp. Many people greeted her as they made their way up the street. They had walked for only a few minutes when they reached a dilapidated barn on the outskirts of the camp.

"This used to be a tobacco barn," said Mrs. Prue. "It's dry, if nothing else."

**Feeding contraband children in
Hilton Head, South Carolina**

Harper's Weekly, June 14, 1862;
courtesy of the Casemate Museum, Fort Monroe

In front of the barn, there was a fire burning. A group of women stood nearby, talking. "Josephine," said Mrs. Prue to one of the women, "I need your help."

A short, plump, cheerful-looking woman left the others and walked toward them. "You know I'm always glad to help," Josephine said, as she joined them.

"We have two new arrivals, Louisa Adams and Lottie Shadwell," Mrs. Prue said, cutting short the introductions. "Will you mark them out a place?" Mrs. Prue took a thick piece of chalk from her pocket and gave it to Josephine.

"Come with me," Josephine said. "You need to see where you're going to be."

It took Lottie's eyes a few minutes to adjust to the dim light inside the barn. She saw four men sitting on the floor playing cards, and three women talking while small children played nearby. "About fifty people live in the barn," Mrs. Prue offered. "More than half of them are children. So Lottie will have playmates."

Lottie looked around and didn't see anyone her age. But it was a sunny day, and she guessed that the older children were enjoying the chance to play outside.

Josephine studied the dirt floor. Everywhere there were chalk circles. She walked around and then squatted and drew another circle. "This will be your place," she told Weza. "Since there are only two of you, this should be big enough."

Weza laughed. "Well, I never could have even imagined such a thing," she said.

"We've had to do this because it's so crowded," Mrs. Prue explained.

"You can leave your things inside the circle," said Josephine. "No one will bother them."

"Thank you, Josephine," Mrs. Prue said. She turned to Lottie and Weza. "Until you get your feet on the ground, you'll receive one-quarter rations from the government. It isn't much. But it's enough to get along on." Mrs. Prue took a man's watch from her pocket and squinted at it. "I have to get back to the office. I'm sure Josephine can fill you in on anything I've missed."

Mrs. Prue and Josephine left, and Lottie and Weza arranged their few belongings inside their chalk circle. They opened the little bags that Mrs. Prue had given them. Inside each was a small towel, a comb, a bar of soap, and a toothbrush. "Well, I declare," said Weza, holding up her toothbrush. "I've never owned one of these."

"Me neither," said Lottie. "Mama always cleaned my teeth with a rag and ashes from the fireplace."

"No wonder you've got such pretty white teeth," said Weza. She smiled, obviously pleased with her toothbrush. "I don't suppose it would hurt to put ashes on this little brush. I'll ask Josephine."

Chapter 10
Lottie-de-da

"Try on your new dress," said Weza. "We need to see if it fits."

Lottie slipped on the dress from the Missionary Association. Ever since she had first seen it, she had hoped that it wouldn't fit so they could bring it back and get another. "Why, it looks like it was made for you," Weza said as she inspected Lottie.

Lottie's heart sank. "It's ugly," she said, feeling sorry for the girl that had once had to wear the dress before it was given to the Missionary Association.

"It isn't a pretty color," said Weza, thinking that it made Lottie look brown all over. "But it's nice and warm. It's wool."

"Can we bring it back, Weza?"

"We'd have to lie if we did. We'd have to say it didn't fit, and that isn't true." Lottie looked crestfallen. "I'll tell you what," Weza said thoughtfully. "We could make a collar and cuffs for it, out of pretty material. That would brighten it up. And we could take off the collar and cuffs and wash them."

"We could use the material Mama gave me," Lottie said.

"That might be just the thing. I don't think there is enough fabric in that piece for a dress. If we use it for collars and

59

cuffs, there would be quite a bit left over for something else. Maybe an apron or a dress for your doll. After we get settled, I'll borrow scissors and get hold of some white thread. I've got needles," she said, reaching down to the hem of her skirt and turning it over for Lottie to see the needles and pins secured there. "Can you sew?"

"Mama taught me," Lottie said. "She did all the mending for Major and Mrs. Shadwell."

"Your blue dress needs to be patched when we find something suitable to patch it with. Will you wear the new dress in the meantime?" asked Weza.

Lottie looked down at the dreary dress. "I guess I can manage for a few days," she said with resignation.

Josephine returned with her two girls, Betsy and Delia, aged three and five. "I'll introduce you to everyone," she said. "Come along with me." Weza and Lottie followed Josephine. Time and time again, Weza repeated the story of how she and Lottie had escaped. And in turn they listened to other people's stories. "You haven't said how you escaped," Weza said to Josephine when there was a lull in the conversation.

Josephine smiled and said, "Our escape wasn't as exciting as yours. We had been planning to escape for months. Then the Confederate army took my husband away to work on Rebel fortifications. We went through with the plan anyway. One night when there was no moon, Ned, my eldest, stole a leaky, flat-bottomed fishing boat from the wharf at Sewell's Point. He rowed me and the girls across Hampton Roads. He rowed all night to get us here to Fortress Monroe and freedom. It rained and we got drenched, but we made it. Ned was so wore out afterwards, he slept for two days straight." Josephine looked around and called to a boy who had just entered the barn. "Ned, come over here. I want you to meet the new folks."

A boy about Lottie's age with skin like black satin and almond-shaped eyes came over to where they sat. He was wearing tattered pants, an oversized shirt, and a blue soldier's kepi. "This is Weza and Lottie," Josephine said.

Ned swept off his hat and bowed from the waist, flashing them a bright smile that lit up his face. Turning to Lottie, he said, "Some of us are going outside for a game. Do you want to come?" Lottie self-consciously looked down at her ugly dress, wishing that she was wearing anything else.

Before she could reply, Weza said with a wave of her hand, "Go along with the others, Lottie. You've heard enough horror stories for now."

Lottie was reluctant to leave Weza and go off with this strange boy. But she did as she was told, following Ned as he bounded toward the door.

Two boys and a girl were milling about near the barn, waiting for Ned. "This is Lottie, she's new," he said as they approached. "What are we going to play?"

A light-skinned girl with her hair in short curls tossed her head impudently. "We've already decided to play underground railroad," said the girl. She turned to Lottie. "My name is Phoebe."

"Do you know how to play?" Ned asked Lottie.

Lottie shook her head. "Someone is the slaver," said Ned. "Others are escaped slaves. It's like hide-and-seek, only better."

It sounded like an awful game to Lottie. She didn't want to play. She didn't want to leave the protective shelter of the barn. She knew she should say something, tell them it was a stupid game, but she was overcome with shyness. She turned and ran back inside.

"What's wrong with her?" asked Ned, clearly puzzled by Lottie's behavior.

Phoebe said, "She's too good to play with us."

Inside the barn, Weza was learning everything she could from Josephine. "There's not much work," Josephine said. "The army hires some freedmen and women. Men earn eight dollars per month, women only four. And the workers rarely get paid. I don't think the army would hire a white-haired woman and scrawny girl. They don't hire women with small children."

"Do the children attend school?" Weza asked remembering something Ida had told them that first day after their rescue.

"Children and adults, too," said Josephine. "The American Missionary Association is opening a new school this spring in the burned-out Hampton Courthouse. Freedmen are working now to rebuild it."

"We're in the right place," said Weza with a satisfied smile. "We'll do just fine here."

In the days that followed, Lottie stayed close to Weza. One Sunday, Ned at his mother's urging, approached Lottie.

"We all have collections," he explained. "We collect Minié balls, belt buckles, uniform buttons, all kinds of army things. We're going to look for some this afternoon. Would you like to come?"

Lottie wanted to go with the others, wanted to be part of their group. But she was afraid, afraid to leave the safety of Grand Contraband Camp. "Where are you going?" she asked timidly.

"Oh, up the road a way and then into the woods," said Ned casually. "I heard there was a skirmish not far from here several months ago. Maybe we'll find bullets and stuff left from the fight."

Lottie thought of the snowy field with its hastily buried bodies where Weza had found the knife blade. "I'd rather not," she said. Before she could explain or even murmur her thanks for the invitation, Ned was off to meet the others. Lottie realized he was relieved that she wasn't coming along.

Lottie joined Ned's two little sisters, Betsy and Delia. They were making mud pies near the barn door, and she sat down next to them. She put her hand into a puddle and pulled out a handful of mud, beginning her own pie. She didn't notice Weza watching her.

The next day, Weza borrowed scissors and thread from Mrs. Prue. "I'll make a pattern and cut out the collar and cuffs," Weza told Lottie when they were back at the barn. "But you'll have to sew them."

Lottie was glad for the chore, for anything that would take her mind off the terrible sadness she felt. She thought of

Mama constantly, her heart aching. Lottie wanted to tell Mama everything, about Weza and their escape, about the barn, and about the children her age and her failure to make friends. "Oh, Mama, will I ever see you again?" she whispered to herself.

When Lottie had been sewing several days, Weza asked, "How are you coming along?"

"I can't make small, neat stitches like Mama taught me," Lottie said. "I don't know what has happened to me."

"The light in this barn is pretty dim. Do the best you can," said Weza soothingly.

Finally, Lottie brought the collar and cuffs to Weza. "I'm finished," she said.

"And you've done a fine job," said Weza, inspecting her work. "We'll put them on the dress right now and we'll use some of the scraps of your material to make hair ties."

After they finished attaching the collar and cuffs to the dress, Lottie stood still while Weza freshly braided her hair and then secured the braids with pink ties. "You look mighty pretty, honey," Weza said, standing back to admire their handiwork. She knew that Lottie must begin to do things by herself. "Could you return the scissors and thread to Mrs. Prue? I'm afraid we've kept them too long."

Lottie dreaded going out alone. She had not forgotten what Mrs. Prue had told them about former slaves being kidnaped. "I guess so," she said, biting her lip.

Lottie went out into the bright sunshine. Mrs. Prue's office wasn't far, and it was a nice day. She wore her coat since it was still cold, but she left it open as she walked so that she wouldn't have to cover up her new collar. When she reached the office, she knocked tentatively on the door.

"Come in," a voice called. Lottie opened the door. The office was full of new arrivals, and Mrs. Prue had her arms full of blankets. "I'm returning these from Weza," Lottie said uncertainly.

"Just put them on the desk," Mrs. Prue said.

Lottie put the scissors and thread on the desk and murmured, "Thank you, ma'am." She gratefully slipped out the door and began walking toward the barn.

Lottie hadn't gone far when she saw some children approaching. She recognized Ned's blue kepi.

"Well if it isn't Lottie-de-da," called out Phoebe when they drew near. She put one hand on her hip and the other behind her head, swiveling her hips as she walked. "Lottie-de-da thinks she's a lady. Lottie-de-da is only a baby." The others picked up the chant. "Lottie-de-da thinks she's a lady."

Lottie felt her cheeks grow hot. She hung her head and walked on, not looking at the others. She wanted to run to Weza and to tell her how mean Ned and his friends were. But Lottie was too embarrassed to say anything to anybody. If only Mama was here, she'd know what to do.

That evening when Lottie was sleeping, Weza and Josephine sat talking. "I'm worried about Lottie," Weza confided in a hushed voice. "The child's almost always by herself. And she's so sad."

"I encouraged Ned to ask Lottie to play with him and the others. But she refused."

"I appreciate what you've done, Josephine," said Weza. "I didn't know Lottie before January. My guess is that she's shy and quiet by nature. Separation from her mother and all we've been through hasn't helped her to gain confidence."

"Maybe when she starts school, she'll do better," suggested Josephine.

"I sure hope so," said Weza with a sigh. She was concerned about Lottie, but she was only one of the things troubling Weza.

Chapter 11

Mr. Meyer

"It feels like spring today," Lottie said, one Saturday morning in early March. She and Weza had finished their breakfast and washed their mess kits.

"Sit for a minute," Weza said, indicating a bench apart from the others. "There's something I want to talk with you about."

Lottie sat down beside Weza, wondering why she seemed so serious. "Some people have been living in this old barn for months," Weza said. "I don't want to do that. I intend to get work and find us a better place to live."

"What will you do?" asked Lottie, thinking about the overcrowded camp with so many freed slaves looking for work. She had sat quietly while Weza talked with the others, and Lottie knew that a recurring subject of conversation was the lack of work.

"I'll do what I've always done...laundry," said Weza. "I've washed clothes for forty-five years, for generations of the Carter family on their place near Williamsburg. There's nothing about laundry I don't know."

"But you don't have any washtubs," Lottie said, hitting immediately on Weza's biggest problem. "There's only one tub here for the whole barn."

"I'm going to see what I can do, starting this morning," Weza said. "Come along. I'm going to talk to the sutlers."

Lottie had seen the sutlers' wagons. Most of them were like traveling general stores. They sold a little bit of everything from canned goods and sewing notions to Bibles and playing cards. Mules moved the wagons from place to place, and there were a half dozen that frequented Fortress Monroe, Grand Contraband Camp, and the hospitals that had sprung up in the area.

They walked for ten minutes before they spotted one near the wharf. Weza approached the wagon. Lottie's attention was riveted immediately by a shelf on which there were jars of candy containing licorice twists, striped peppermints, lemon drops, and maple sugar squares. Weza's glance took in the bolts of gingham, spools of thread, and cooking utensils before coming to rest on a washboard and a pail.

"Can I help you, ladies?" asked the man in charge of the wagon. He was a short, fat man with pink and white skin and squinty blue eyes.

"I'm looking for a washtub," said Weza.

"The best I can do is that pail and washboard," the man replied. "You can have both for a dollar."

"I've got no dollar," Weza said, thinking that the price was high. "Is there any chance of getting the pail and washboard on time?"

"I don't give credit to you people," the man said. "It don't pay because you don't pay." Weza held her head high and glared at the man. She said nothing. She turned and walked away.

Weza and Lottie went from sutler to sutler, getting pretty much the same answer everywhere they went. The sutlers didn't carry washtubs, and the pails and washboards they had were all outrageously expensive. And no one was willing to let Weza pay for a pail and washboard on time.

By noon, they had walked many miles and were discouraged and footsore. There was only one sutler's wagon that they hadn't approached. The man who owned this last wagon had a bad reputation. He was ill-tempered, brusque, and a Jew, the freed slaves had warned Weza. They told her that if there was any man who pinched every penny until it cried, it was Amos Meyer.

When they spotted his wagon, Lottie was surprised. "You're not going to ask him?" she said.

"I might as well," Weza said. "His refusal will be no worse than the rest. Besides, maybe he gets asked for things like this less often."

Lottie followed Weza with some misgivings. Lottie had seen the grizzled, old man around the camp. He always wore a black suit and a curious, little round cap on his gray, wiry hair. She had no idea what a Jew was. But from the tone of voice the slaves used, she guessed it wasn't something good.

Weza approached the sutler. He was bent over his account book. He peered up at Weza through thick glasses. "Yes," he said. "May I help you?" His words were polite, and yet his manner was wary.

"I've noticed you around camp, Mr. Meyer," Weza began a bit hesitantly. "And you always wear a white shirt." The sutler snapped his head up from his account book, more interested now. Why had this woman noticed what he wore? Weza continued, "I am wondering if you have anyone who does your washing. If not, I'd like the job."

The sutler was relieved that the woman only wanted work. "How much would you charge?" he asked.

"Well sir, I'm not sure," Weza said. "I'm just going into business and...," she hesitated, "and I don't have a washtub or a washboard. If you would be willing to let me buy these things on time, I'd wash your clothes at no charge until I pay you back." Mr. Meyer didn't say anything, and Weza went on. "Once I got them paid for, I'd do your laundry at a reduced rate."

Mr. Meyer still didn't say anything. He was thinking about how he would have to get a washtub from his supplier and how, except for the free laundry, there will be little profit in the transaction, even with a hefty interest charge. This woman also would need a large kettle to boil water to kill lice. Vermin were a continual problem throughout the camp. And she'd need two irons. Shirts had to be ironed. If she was going to make a success of her business, she should do it right. And if she did it right, he'd get his money back. Unlike some of the other sutlers, he was willing to go to extra trouble to make a small amount of money. He had found over the years that the small amounts added up. And then, too, he hated doing his own laundry. The area around Fortress Freedom was dirty, and it was difficult for him, living in his wagon as he did, to keep himself clean. It would be a help to have a capable woman do the laundry.

Lottie shifted from one foot to the other while Weza stood patiently waiting for the sutler to reply. "It will take me a while to get a suitable washtub," he said, scribbling some figures in his account book. "It will cost you two dollars for a tub and washboard. Plus you'll need irons, soap, and clothesline. You should have a kettle also or you won't kill the graybacks. Let me see. The cost to you will be four dollars, the total due in four months. Is that agreeable?"

"Yes, sir," Weza said in her most businesslike manner. She knew it was a lot of money. But it was the chance she had been looking for.

"Come back in two weeks. I'll have your tub by then," he said, again bending over his books. Weza didn't move. He looked up and asked, "Is that all?"

"One other thing," said Weza. "We're living right now in that old tobacco barn near Lincoln Street. If you hear about any other place that might do for us, we'd appreciate it if you let us know. That old barn isn't the best place to do laundry."

"I deal with a lot of people each day. If I hear anything, I'll keep you in mind," the sutler said, turning again to concentrate on his accounts.

Weza and Lottie left, and the sutler never looked up. When they were well out of his hearing, Weza said, "In this life, you often don't know who your friends are."

"But he isn't our friend," Lottie said. "He didn't even nod goodbye."

"He didn't smile and slap us on the back," said Weza. "But he's the only sutler in this whole place to give us what we wanted and needed."

"He just wants his laundry done for free," said Lottie.

"That's all right. There's nothing wrong with wanting to be clean."

Chapter 12

The Turtle and the Cheese Box

"It's a struggle to keep clean in this old barn," said Weza. She and Lottie had been waiting all morning to have their turn at the bathtub. On Saturdays, the women placed it in back of the barn. They strung blankets on ropes around it so that they could bathe in privacy. Weza and Lottie had finished their noon meal, and it was finally their turn to wash when they heard a booming noise. Other loud crashes followed.

People began running in the direction of the noise. Amid the commotion, a boy ran past Lottie and Weza. "What's that?" Weza called out.

The boy kept running and shouted over his shoulder, "Some kind of fight! Out on the water!"

A soldier hurried by the barn. "Can you tell us what's going on?" Weza asked.

"A naval battle! A Rebel ship is on a rampage," he said abruptly and continued on his way.

"Can we go see?" asked Lottie.

After waiting all morning for the bathtub, Weza hesitated for a moment. Just then, Josephine ran up. She was carrying Betsy and leading Delia by the hand. "There's a battle out on the water. Ned's out there! He went fishing, and he hasn't come back. Come with me to the waterfront!"

"All right," said Weza. She reached out for Betsy. "Lottie, take Delia's hand."

The two women and the children made their way with many others to the waterfront.

"I smell smoke," Lottie said as they headed toward the fortress. The smell of smoke grew stronger as they neared the water.

"My goodness," said Weza. "I've never seen so many boats." The water was filled with small steamboats, rowboats, and sailboats. Two large vessels nearby were getting up steam and clouds of black smoke poured from their funnels. Shore batteries began firing at a squat, strange-looking ship in the distance, but it kept coming toward them. It began firing at a Union ship with tall masts. They heard the howling of shells, followed by explosions when they hit their mark.

"It's an ironclad, the *Virginia*. The *Congress* is getting pounded," they heard someone say.

"Ned's out there in all that!" Josephine wailed. She stood on her tiptoes and scanned the horizon. "Why hasn't he come back?"

"Now, don't worry about Ned," said Weza. "Those naval officers have got more on their minds just now than a boy in an old rowboat."

"The *Cumberland*'s being rammed," they heard a man with a telescope say. Lottie craned her neck, but she couldn't tell what was happening. She did see little black spots that turned into white clouds of smoke.

The shore was crowded with spectators and except for occasional comments an unusual quiet fell over those who had gathered. "The rowboat's green," said Josephine almost in a whisper.

A while later, someone said, "The Rebel ship is shelling the *Congress* again." Lottie saw flames shooting into the air and black billowing smoke. Something exploded aboard the ship and the flames leapt higher and the smoke grew blacker.

It was late afternoon when small boats began bringing ashore the wounded from the stricken Union ships. Hospital ambulances were lined up along the wharf.

Josephine was anxious. "Where is he?" she asked scanning the horizon again.

"Ned can take care of himself," said Weza.

Josephine continued to study the little boats coming and going on the water. "I think I see him," said Josephine, a little while later. "There, look! Next to the sailboat!"

A small dark shape was pulling steadily on the oars of a green rowboat. As they watched, the boat slowly came closer. "He's got somebody in the boat. Somebody hurt!" said Josephine.

Lottie could see Ned's kepi now. It bobbed back and forth as he bent to the oars.

Ned rowed directly to the wharf. Several other boats were discharging wounded, and he had to wait his turn.

Chapter 12

Weza and Josephine and the children edged through the crowd and got to the wharf in time to see strong arms help the wounded sailor from Ned's boat. "Good job, sonny," they heard one man say. Ned found a place where he could tie his boat and came ashore.

Josephine rushed to Ned and threw her arms around him. "Oh, Ned, are you all right?"

"I'm all right," he said. "I'm not so sure about the sailor I hauled out of the water."

"How did you happen to pick him up?" Josephine asked. "I've been so worried about you. You've been gone so long. I was afraid something happened to you."

"An officer on one of the small steamers went around asking all the small boats out on the water to help with the wounded. I'm sorry, Mama. I knew you'd be worried, but I couldn't very well leave when I might help someone."

Josephine gave Ned another hug and when she let him go, Weza asked, "Are we in any danger?" A number of people nearby turned to listen to Ned.

"Things aren't looking good for the Union fleet. That Rebel ship, the *Virginia*, has iron sides. Our cannon shot just bounced off. One of the boatmen told me that the *Virginia* can't be stopped. She has sunk the *Cumberland*. Her masts are sticking out of the water like dead trees in a swamp. The *Congress* is burning and the big Union steamship, the *Minnesota*, is aground." Ned paused for a moment, enjoying the attention of the little group gathered around him. Then he continued, "There's talk of the Confederates under

General Magruder attacking by land from the north. If that happens, we'll be cut off."

Lottie had made a point of avoiding Ned ever since he and the other children had made fun of her brown dress. But now, she, like everyone else, hung on his words. She noticed that Ned's hands were bloody. He had rowed until his hands bled.

A bald man began questioning Ned, and Lottie turned to Weza. "Are the Confederates going to attack Fortress Freedom and make us slaves again?" she asked, biting her lip.

Weza frowned and shook her head. "It doesn't seem likely, what with all the soldiers here," she said. She was uneasy, but she tried to sound confident for Lottie's sake.

That evening after a cold, hurried supper of dried beef and biscuits, they returned to the shore to watch the *Congress* burn. The whole sky was lit with an eery reddish glow. Flames engulfed the *Congress* and occasionally shot high in the air. Suddenly, there was a huge bang as something exploded. A great pillar of flame rose from the ship and was obscured moments later by thick smoke.

Weza and Lottie slept poorly that night. Everyone was worried about what the next day would bring. In the morning, the tobacco barn was abuzz with excitement. "What now?" Weza asked Josephine when she joined the women at the cookfire in front of the barn.

"Another fight has started. The *Virginia*'s come back to finish off the *Minnesota*. We're all going to the waterfront."

"We'll come along, too," Weza said.

Battle of the *Monitor* and *Virginia*, March 9, 1862

Courtesy of Casemate Museum, Fort Monroe

Ned went with them today, bouncing along happily as if he was going to a picnic. When they got to the waterfront, he scurried off to find out the latest news.

All Lottie could see were two distant specks out on the water. There were occasional flashes of fire, followed by plumes of smoke. And the awful noise.

Ned returned a few moments later. "Today the Union has an ironclad, too! It arrived last night. Its name's the *Monitor*. Everybody's calling it the *Cheese Box* because it looks like a round cheese box on a board. They're calling the Rebel ironclad, the *Turtle*. They found out yesterday that she's slow and has a tough shell." Lottie squinted, trying to see the ships more clearly.

"Who's winning?" asked Weza.

"It's hard to say," said Ned. "The *Turtle* went after the *Minnesota*. But the little *Cheese Box* drove her off. I heard that the *Turtle*'s going to attack Washington and then New York."

"There are always rumors at times like this," said Weza, putting her arm reassuringly about Lottie's shoulders.

For a long time they watched the distant battle. By suppertime, the word spread that the *Turtle* had crawled away, thanks to the feisty little *Cheese Box*. The danger had passed, at least for now.

The following morning everyone went again to the waterfront. This time they went to see the *Cheese Box* steam by the fortress. As the funny little ironclad came near, the crowd cheered wildly.

"I declare," said Weza, "that boat does look just like a cheese box."

Chapter 13

A Shanty with a Chimney

The following week, Weza and Lottie again sought out Mr. Meyer. They found him near the fortress. Several blue-uniformed soldiers were inspecting Mr. Meyer's goods. One bought a special lice comb for ten cents and another a pocket mirror for twenty cents. When they were through, Lottie and Weza approached the wagon. Mr. Meyer reached inside and produced a big kettle, a washtub, and a washboard. Without a word, he took two irons, a bar of yellow soap, and a length of rope for clothesline from where they were displayed with the other sundries. He wrapped them in a piece of brown paper and put the package into the washtub along with a bundle of dirty laundry, neatly tied up in a shirt.

"Thank you," Weza said as he handed it to her. "I'll have your clean laundry day after tomorrow."

Mr. Meyer nodded. Then almost as an afterthought, he said, "A man mentioned that the government was letting his family have land to farm. They're leaving here. I asked if they lived in a shanty and he said yes. When I asked what he would take for it, he seemed surprised. He hadn't thought of selling it, he said, since he didn't rightly own it. I explained that I knew a woman and a child that needed a place to live.

Well, he hemmed and hawed saying that he knew somebody else who wanted it. I said that you would give him five dollars for the place if it was decent at all."

"And where would I get five dollars?" Weza asked.

"We'll worry about that if the place is suitable and if he hasn't already given it to someone else," Mr. Meyer said. "Go and ask to see the place. Tell them I sent you."

The sutler gave Weza directions, and a half-hour later, they were back at Grand Contraband Camp, looking for the shanty. It had been built on the ruins of one of the houses in Hampton that the Rebels burned when they retreated. The builder had butted the shanty right up to the old fireplace so it could be used for cooking and heating. With the tall chimney towering over it, the shanty was easy to spot. Weza went to the door and knocked.

"Mr. Meyer sent me," she told the young woman who opened the door. The woman was tall with red-brown skin and high cheekbones.

"My husband isn't here, but come on in," the woman said.

There was only one room, but the shanty had a loft and two windows. The furniture consisted of a rough table with two benches, two shelves on one wall, and a string bed in the corner of the room. A toddler played on the floor in front of the fireplace, and a baby slept in a packing box on the table. "We're taking the pallet and my few dishes and pans," the woman said. "My husband says we can't take the rest. If you want the place, you're welcome to whatever we can't carry."

"It looks to be a pretty snug shanty," Weza said, trying not to show her excitement. "Where do you get your water?"

"There's a well just over there," the woman pointed through the front window. "We had water last summer even during the hottest months. My Henry built this place, and we wouldn't leave here except that he's hankering after some land where we can farm. A man has to work for himself, he says. And he's tired of waiting for the army to pay him."

Weza studied every aspect of the shanty. It would be ideal for her and Lottie. If only she could find a way to get it. "I'll be back to see you tomorrow," she told the woman as they were leaving. "I'll let you know then if we are interested in the place."

Early the next morning, they were at Mr. Meyer's wagon when he opened the sides to do business. Weza told him about the shanty, carefully describing its advantages. "Having a well so close would be a great help with the laundry," she concluded.

"I will lend you the five dollars," Mr. Meyer said. "You'll pay me back seven dollars, one dollar a month. Since you already have borrowed four dollars, all together you will owe me a dollar a month for the next eleven months. And as part of our deal, I'll expect free laundry."

Weza hesitated for only a moment. Eleven dollars sounded like a lot of money when she didn't have a copper to her name. But it was an opportunity that she couldn't afford to pass up. "Free laundry only until my debt is paid," she said.

"You have the making of a good businesswoman," Mr. Meyer said. He handed her five dollars and wrote down the total in his account book.

Three days later, Lottie and Weza moved out of the tobacco barn and into the shanty. "Fortunately, we didn't have much to take with us," Lottie said, looking around their new home and surveying the few things given to them by the Missionary Association.

"And the shanty is clean," said Weza. "We can begin trying to find laundry customers right away."

"How will we do that?" Lottie asked, hoping she would not have to approach people and ask if they needed their laundry done.

"We'll ask around at the Saturday market. Everybody goes there to buy or sell: soldiers, townspeople, tradesmen, everybody. I don't think it'll be difficult."

Weza was right as usual. On Saturday, she walked up to an overweight woman selling preserves at the market and asked, "Ma'am, I'm taking in washing. Would you be interested?"

Lottie was surprised when the woman first looked confused and then stammered out, "Yes, in fact, I need help with my laundry. I live on Page Street, the second house on the right. Come by tomorrow, and we'll talk."

There were a great number of soldiers milling about. Weza and Lottie approached four young men who were in the process of dividing up a homemade chess pie with a bayonet. "I'm taking in laundry," Weza said. "Would any of you want your clothes washed?"

"Yes, ma'am," said one young soldier enthusiastically, "if I miss anything more than home cooking, it's having somebody do my laundry."

"That goes for me, too," said another soldier. "We're from Ohio, and our encampment isn't far from here."

Weza arranged to visit them tomorrow after she saw the woman on Page Street. "It will be midmorning," she told them.

Lottie was glad that she was not the one who had to ask strangers if they needed their laundry done. It didn't seem to bother Weza, and Lottie was surprised that in no time at all Weza had as much business as she could handle. "That was easier than I thought it would be," Lottie said, as they were heading home.

"It's easy to sell something that people want. And with all the mud around here, I just knew people would want their clothes washed," said Weza.

Chapter 14
Love Is Strong

Woman doing laundry with a small girl boiling clothes

"Where do you get your energy?" Lottie asked Weza one day several weeks later. They had just finished hanging up a big batch of laundry, and Weza was getting ready to iron shirts.

"This is the first time in my life that I've worked for myself," said Weza. "And I'm determined to make a success of it. It's been a long day. Why don't you go out and play for a while?"

"I don't mind the work," Lottie said, sitting down at their table. "Let me fold some things for you." Lottie picked up the linens they had washed the day before. "When I'm busy, I miss Mama less. And...."

Weza sat down on the bench beside her. "And what?"

Lottie hesitated, and then blurted out, "And I don't feel so left out. The others never ask me to play."

"You got off on the wrong foot making friends," Weza said. "But one of these days, you'll find a friend. All you really need is one good friend. After that, it won't be so difficult to make other friends. When someone becomes your friend, the rest will follow. You'll see. Right now, we've no time for anything but laundry if we're to pay Mr. Meyer his dollar at the end of the month."

The following morning, Lottie rose before dawn. The sky was still blue-black, but in the east it was getting light. Weza was already outside where she was starting a fire under their big kettle. "There's cornbread and coffee for breakfast," said Weza. "After you've eaten, you'll have to find some wood. Our supply's running low."

"Yes, ma'am," said Lottie. She hated looking for wood. It meant that she left the safety of Weza and the shanty. Each day, it was necessary for her to go further and further from home to find enough wood to heat the wash water and do their cooking.

Lottie ate the cornbread and washed it down with the tepid chicory coffee. Then she left to look for wood. "I hope to be back soon," she told Weza as she headed off toward the center of camp.

Many people were still asleep, and the camp was quiet. She passed a group of men with shovels accompanied by two soldiers. They were walking in the direction of the fortress. She'd been looking for wood for twenty minutes when she passed a sutler's wagon. The sutler was outside feeding his mules. Lottie stopped for a moment to watch. Not far from the wagon, she spotted a broken, wooden box that was half-hidden in some brush near the road. Somebody probably had bought something from the sutler, broken open the box, and then discarded the packaging. "I'm in luck today," she said to herself. She picked it up. It was heavy and would burn for a while. She headed home, stopping occasionally to put down the box and rest her arms. She got back in time to help Weza rinse the morning's wash. She drew three pails of water from the well and then swished the clothes that Weza had washed.

"I'd sure like to have leek soup," Weza said, after they had finished the rinsing and hung out the clothes to dry. "I'll go and see if any of the farmers who have set up market stalls today have any leeks. Take a break and play for a while."

Lottie placed the clothes basket back on its hook. She'd rather go with Weza, but her tone of voice didn't encourage any questioning. "All right," Lottie said, "I'll just get Bebe."

Weza put on a fresh bandana and picked up her shopping basket. She gave Lottie a hug. "I'll be back soon," Weza said as she headed toward the center of camp. As she left, she saw Lottie settling herself with her doll near the rag pile. Weza washed and saved any old rags she or Lottie found. The ragman came by twice a week and gave her a few pennies for the rags. The rag pile had become a favorite place for Lottie to play with her doll. For Lottie the old rags became capes, gowns, tents, bandages, and even swaddling clothes.

Weza looked back at Lottie, talking softly to her doll. Playing all by herself, she seemed small and defenseless. It was hard to leave her alone even for a short time, but Weza knew that she had to help Lottie become more independent. "That child still pulls at my heartstrings," she mumbled as she headed down the road.

That night at supper, Lottie suddenly noticed that Bebe wasn't in her usual place on the little shelf by the fireplace. "Have you seen Bebe?" Lottie asked Weza who was serving her a bowl of steaming leek soup.

"No, child, I haven't," said Weza. "Maybe you left her outside. Eat your dinner, then go take a look."

Lottie usually dawdled during meals. Tonight she ate quickly and ran outside looking for Bebe. A moment later she was back. "Bebe isn't there," she said. "And the rags are all gone, too."

"It was Rastus' day to pick up rags. I saw him when I was coming back from the farmer's market, and he paid me. "Could you," Weza stopped in mid sentence, " have left Bebe in the rag pile?"

Lottie bit her lip. "Oh, no!" she said with tears brimming at her eyes. "Oh, Weza, what can I do?"

Weza got up and began clearing away their dinner plates. "Check the shanty while I clean up."

"Bebe's not here," Lottie said a few minutes later. "I've looked everywhere."

"You'll have to find the ragman and get Bebe back," Weza said, taking off her apron.

"I'll never find him," Lottie said. "We have no idea where he lives." She sat down at the table, put her head down, and buried her face under her arms.

"Do you love that doll?" Weza asked.

Lottie raised her head, revealing tear-stained cheeks. "You know I do, Weza! Mama made her for me!"

"Well, then?" Weza said. "How can you give her up so easily?"

"Will you come with me, Weza?" Lottie asked.

"Of course I will," Weza said. "But, it's your doll and your fault she's lost. So, you'll have to do the asking and the finding."

"I'm not sure I can do it," said Lottie. "I'm not brave like you, Weza."

"What ever gives you that idea? You've said that to me before," said Weza.

"I'm like Mama."

"What do you mean?"

"Did you know Mama cried and threw herself around Major Shadwell's knees when he told her that I was to be sold?"

"So?"

"Mama begged him not to separate us! Begged him...on her knees."

Weza sighed. "Child, everyone does the best they can. Your mama must have known that the only hope was to appeal to the man's feelings. My way has always been different. But that doesn't make it right. I told you I was sold because I was too old. That's only half the story. I've always said my piece. Spoke my mind. My recklessness got me branded as a troublemaker."

"But Weza, it was awful to see Mama beg. She seemed so...so weak."

"*He* was awful." Weza paused. Then she continued. "You told me your mama found you a warm coat the night before you left. How did she do that? What did she have to sell or promise in order to get that coat for you?"

Lottie thought back to the last night she spent in Williamsburg. Mama had gone out in the evening and taken with her the friendship garden quilt she had worked on for years. At the time, Lottie hadn't thought anything of it. Suddenly, she realized what the warm coat had cost her mother. "People were always asking to see Mama's prized quilt," she said. "I never realized until now that she must have traded it for my coat. All I remember is that when she came back, she was happy to have found me a coat."

"Just as I thought. Your mama is strong because love is strong, the strongest thing there is," said Weza. "Now come on. We're wasting time."

Chapter 15

Talking to Strangers

Lottie and Weza headed toward the center of Grand Contraband Camp where the market stalls were closing for the day. They saw a dark-skinned peddler loading produce he had not sold onto a wagon. Weza nodded in the man's direction. "Ask him if he's seen Rastus?" she said, standing to one side.

Lottie looked pleadingly at Weza. "Please, won't you do it for me?"

Weza shook her head. "It's important that you ask him," she said.

Lottie walked toward the man. He picked up a box of cabbages and slung it onto the wagon. She swallowed and bit her lip as she approached. She was not sure she could speak to a complete stranger who was obviously busy. "Excuse me, sir," she said finally, in such a little voice that she wasn't sure he heard her.

The man stopped work and turned in her direction. Lottie moved back a step or two. The man raised his bushy eyebrows, waiting for her to speak again.

Lottie looked down at her bare feet. "Please sir," she said after a moment. "Have you seen Rastus?"

"Not as I can recall today," he said. "Sorry." He glanced at Weza and picked up a bag of potatoes.

Lottie retreated to Weza's side. "Did I do all right?"

"You did just fine. Although you should look at people when you talk to them. You're not a slave anymore. Slaves look at their feet. And you need to speak up."

It became a little easier as they went on for Lottie to ask about Rastus. Finally, a bent old woman sitting outside a shanty, chewing tobacco, helped them. "No, I haven't seen him today," she said, sending a stream of tobacco juice into the weeds near her feet. "But I know he lives somewhere down by the water. That way." She pointed a bony finger in the opposite direction from the way they were walking.

Thanking the old lady, Lottie and Weza headed in the direction of the waterfront. Weza usually avoided this part of the camp in the evening. It was a rough section, filled with gambling dens, dance halls, and shot houses where whiskey was sold by the drink.

They slowed as they neared the waterfront. The streets were filled with off-duty soldiers, and foot-stomping, fiddle music came from a sizeable, unpainted building. Looking about uncertainly, Lottie finally approached a heavily rouged young woman sauntering along the street in high-heeled shoes. Her hair was piled high on her head and she wore a tight, red skirt.

"Rastus?" the woman replied to Lottie's question. "That old scumbag lives around here somewhere."

Lottie must have looked crestfallen because the woman thought better of her flip attitude and added, "Go to the end of the street. Turn to the right." The woman hurried away before Lottie could thank her.

They followed the woman's directions and after turning the corner, they spotted Rastus' mule. The worn-looking, ancient animal was unmistakable. It stood in a little fenced area near a dilapidated shanty with a roof made of tent canvas.

As they approached, Rastus came around the corner of the building. He had once been a doorman at a restaurant, and he wore a well-cut black suit that had grown shabby and dirty from constant wear. When he saw them, he took off his battered top hat, revealing white, wooly hair. He bowed slightly. "Miss Weza," he said, "to what do I owe the pleasure of seeing you twice in the same day?"

"Lottie here has something to ask you," said Weza.

Lottie took a deep breath. She explained, as best she could, how her doll might have gotten mixed up with the rags he had picked up from their shanty. She ended by asking, "May I look for Bebe in the rag pile?"

Rastus looked into Lottie's stricken face. "All the stuff I got today is over there in the cart," he said in his deep, steady voice. "You go right ahead and look. It may take a while. I had a good day today." He turned to Weza. "And while she does that Miss Weza, you sit here on this bench, and I'll be right back. I've got something for you."

It had been a long day. Weza sat down on the bench and eased her feet onto an exposed tree root nearby. Her back ached and her ankles were swollen. It felt good to put her feet up.

Lottie climbed into the rickety little cart and began pawing through the rags. Weza washed all the rags that came their way and now Lottie knew why. Most of the rags were disgusting. Some were damp; others were soiled. Lottie was horrified by the thought that her beloved Bebe might be buried alive under such filth. In the fading daylight, she searched anxiously for her doll.

A moment later, Rastus was back. "I noticed you're starting a garden," he said. "These are for you." He handed Weza a square of cloth. "Hollyhock seeds. I collected them last fall. And I've planted some. But I had extra."

"Why, thank you, Rastus," said Weza, surprised and pleased. "I'm going to put in a few vegetables. I dearly love flowers, but I didn't think we could afford any seeds this year. Hollyhocks will brighten up our place."

While Weza chatted with Rastus about her garden plans, Lottie continued to look through the rags. She was becoming disheartened when she thought she recognized a scrap of yellowed linen, part of a discarded tablecloth that she had played with earlier in the day. Her heart pounded. She still didn't see Bebe, and Lottie was almost at the bottom of the pile. She gave a little cry. There was Bebe.

Lottie pulled the doll from the rags and clenched Bebe to her chest in a long hug. Bebe was dirty, but she was all right.

Lottie leapt from the wagon and ran to Weza. "I've found her," Lottie said, holding out the doll at arm's length for Weza to inspect.

Weza examined Bebe. The doll looked more bedraggled than usual from her hours in the rag cart. "Bebe, it's time you had a new dress," Weza said to the doll. "We'll make one out of that pretty pink material Lottie's mama gave her."

Weza struggled to her feet. "Thank you for the seeds, Rastus," she said, "and for letting Lottie recover her doll."

Rastus grinned, revealing a huge gap between his front teeth. "You come see old Rastus anytime," he said.

Lottie held Bebe close to her as they walked back toward their shanty in the gathering darkness. Lottie was happy to have her doll back. The discomfort she had experienced talking to strangers was forgotten.

"I'm worn out," Weza said as they neared home. "Do you think you could deliver and pick up the laundry for me?" she asked.

Before the events of the last several hours, Lottie never would have thought herself capable of such a thing. She looked at Weza whose slow steps revealed her fatigue. "I think so," she said. "I'll try."

"We could take on more work if every afternoon I wasn't traipsing back and forth all over the place," Weza said wearily. She knew that picking up and delivering laundry wouldn't be easy for Lottie. But if she was to survive in the uncertain future, she would need to overcome her feelings of insecurity, and Weza was determined to do everything in her power to help Lottie grow in confidence.

Before Lottie went by herself the first time to return a basket of clean laundry to a Mrs. Collingwood, Weza gave her instructions. "I know you're sometimes bashful, but that's no excuse for not being polite," she said. "Always go to the back door. Look at people when you talk to them. Say 'yes, ma'am' and 'yes, sir.' If they say they can't pay, tell them that you'll take no more of their laundry. When anyone gives you laundry, don't forget to tell them when you'll bring it back. And be sure to say 'thank you.'"

"I don't think Mrs. Collingwood likes us," said Lottie, remembering the times she had gone with Weza to the woman's house. It was one of the houses in Hampton that had not been burned by the Confederate army when they retreated from the city. Mrs. Collingwood always acted as if Weza and Lottie were to blame for the Union occupation of the city.

"She doesn't have to like us. Nor us, her. She just has to pay for the work we've done."

"Can't you go with me, just this time?"

"I could go with you. But I'm not going to. We owe Mr. Meyer money. The more you can help, the sooner we'll be able to pay our debt."

Lottie picked up the basket of Mrs. Collingwood's laundry. "It looks like rain," she said.

"Hurry along and watch the sky. If the old lady's laundry gets wet, she'll throw a fit."

Lottie went out into the gray morning. Dark clouds sat on the western horizon and a fresh breeze blew in from the water. The basket grew heavy as Lottie made her way toward Mrs. Collingwood's house. Yet she felt like she could carry it for miles if only she didn't have to knock on Mrs. Collingwood's door.

The small white house came into view. Lottie slowed her pace, dreading the moment when she had to deal with the old lady. Just then, big raindrops started to fall, and Lottie had no choice but to run to the house. The laundry on top was getting wet. She went around to the back door. Placing the laundry as close as possible to the door, she knocked urgently. The wind blew sheets of rain toward her. She tried to shield the basket with her body.

Mrs. Collingwood lived alone and she moved slowly because of her age and weight. It seemed like a long time before she opened the door. "Come in out of the rain, girl," she said when she saw Lottie.

Lottie picked up the basket and went into the kitchen. She knew she should say something, but she felt paralyzed by the formidable figure before her.

"I see you've managed to get my things wet," Mrs. Collingwood said in her usual abrupt manner.

"I'm sorry," Lottie struggled to say. Then she added, "ma'am." She could feel her eyes fill up with tears of frustration.

"Well, don't carry on about it. Take those wet things and spread them on the chairs near the fire." Mrs. Collingwood pointed to the kitchen chairs with her cane.

Lottie spread the wet clothes on the chairs. Once she got below the top layer, she saw that the sheets weren't wet. "The rest is all right," she managed to say, as she placed the neatly folded sheets on the table.

"Where's the other one today?" asked Mrs. Collingwood.

"I'll be doing deliveries from now on," replied Lottie.

Mrs. Collingwood took out her change purse and counted out ten cents. "What's your name again?" she asked.

"I'm Lottie."

"Well, Lottie, here's my dirty laundry. See that you don't get my clothes wet next time."

"Yes, ma'am," said Lottie, putting the dirty laundry into her basket. "I'll bring it back Wednesday."

Lottie hurried home, paying no attention to the falling rain. She had done it. All by herself, she had managed the transaction with Mrs. Collingwood. Her next customer would be easier.

Chapter 16
She's Mean

**Hampton Courthouse. The man on the roof is
sounding the curfew bell, warning African
Americans that it is bedtime.**

Frank Leslie's *Illustrated Weekly*, August 10, 1861;
courtesy of the Casemate Museum, Fort Monroe

When the new school opened, Weza accompanied Lottie
to the rebuilt courthouse. They entered a large, noisy school
room that smelled of freshly cut lumber. Long lines of children and parents had formed in front of tables at one end of
the room. A teacher sat at each table, taking the names of the

new students. "There will be sixty children in Lottie's class," the teacher said when it came her turn to register for classes. She looked up at Weza. "There are classes for adults. Don't you want to register too?"

"I've got too much work to do, just now," Weza said in her firm, but pleasant way. "Lottie's going to learn for us both."

When they left the school building, Lottie began to have doubts about attending school. "What about my laundry deliveries and pickups?" she asked. "How will we pay Mr. Meyer if I don't help you?"

"You can help me when you're through with your lessons for the day," Weza assured her. "There will always be plenty of work to do. You won't always have the chance to learn."

Lottie was uncomfortable when Weza left her the next day at the school. Lottie entered the building and gave her name to a thin young man who stood near the door. He directed her to a big room beside the one where she had registered. She went inside and stood with other children at the back. A pale, white teacher with sharp features and sand-colored hair pulled back in a bun stood at a kitchen table that served as a desk.

"Everyone sit down," the teacher said, raising her shrill voice. "This is a school room. Not a camp meeting." No one seemed to be listening. She took a ruler from her book bag and banged it on the corner of the table. The squirming children began to find seats. Lottie sat near the back on a rough, unpainted bench with a half-dozen other children.

Teacher holding a sphere during class

Harper's Weekly, February 26, 1870

"My name is Miss Bosworth," the teacher said. "I'm from Massachusetts." There was a map pinned to the wall, and she pointed to the state. "We're here in Virginia."

Lottie looked where Miss Bosworth pointed. "I've been sent to Virginia by the American Missionary Association. I'll expect your cooperation. Anyone who doesn't behave will be asked to leave. There are so many children and adults who want to learn, we've no time to bother with those who don't."

Lottie sat quietly during the next several weeks and took everything in, but whenever the teacher called on her, Lottie never seemed to know the answer. She began to dread going to school. One afternoon, she thought she had escaped being called on when Miss Bosworth said, "Lottie, please sound out the letters on the board."

The Union ABCs illustrate a wartime teaching aid.

Courtesy of The Baldwin Library of Historical Children's Literature, University of Florida

Lottie stood and stared at the makeshift blackboard in the front of the room, biting her bottom lip. She had memorized the alphabet printed in large letters and placed across the front of the room. But she couldn't recognize the letters on the board. She stood there not saying a word, her face growing hot with embarrassment.

"You may sit down, Lottie," said the teacher with a sigh of resignation. She had known that teaching former slaves would be difficult, but each day she learned anew just how great a challenge she had taken on. She nodded to the girl next to Lottie, "Phoebe."

Lottie's acquaintance from the tobacco barn stood without hesitation and easily read the words, "The cat catches the rat." With a satisfied smirk at Lottie, Phoebe sat down. Lottie cringed.

It was warm in the classroom in spite of the high ceilings and long windows opened at the bottom. The teacher looked at the sixty children, all struggling to sit still. "We'll recite the alphabet one more time and the threes table. That will be all for today."

Lottie droned out the alphabet with the others as Miss Bosworth pointed to the large, printed letters. Then she recited the threes table up to thirty as the teacher held up papers with numbers boldly written on them. "Class dismissed," said Miss Bosworth finally. Lottie hurried outside, relieved the lessons were over. She had thought she would like school, but she hated it. She would rather help Weza with the laundry.

As Lottie neared their shanty, she saw Weza outside. The older woman was bent over a washtub. He arms moved up and down rhythmically as she scrubbed a tubful of clothes. She looked up and smiled as Lottie approached. "How did it go today?" she asked.

Lottie choked up. It was important to Weza that Lottie attend school. How could she tell her how she felt about it? Finally, Lottie blurted out, "The teacher called on me again. She calls on me almost every day. And I never know the answer."

"It'll go better tomorrow," Weza said, transferring wet clothes from the wash water to the rinse water. She swished the clothes to get out the soap and then put them into a basket.

"I'll hang those up for you," said Lottie, picking up the basket as Weza finished. She began stringing shirts on the line that reached from their shanty to a nearby sapling. "I'd rather help you than go to school."

Weza straightened up and wiped her hands on her apron. She didn't know what to do. She knew Lottie hated school and wasn't learning.

"What happened today?" Weza asked.

"Phoebe is a showoff," Lottie said stubbornly. "She makes everyone else look stupid."

"Is everyone else stupid?"

"Of course not, just me," Lottie said.

"You're talking trash, again. I want you to go see your teacher for extra help."

Lottie let the shirt she was holding fall back into the basket. "I can't do that," she said.

"And why not?" Weza asked, putting her hands resolutely on her hips.

"She's mean."

"How can you say that? Miss Bosworth isn't like those two polecat slavers. I think you're afraid of her."

Lottie thought for a moment. "I'm not brave like you are, Weza."

Weza threw her hands up in the air. "In the first place, you were every bit as brave as I was when we escaped."

"That's not true, Weza. You're not afraid of anybody, slavers or soldiers, anybody."

"Everybody is afraid sometimes," said Weza. "And back there in the woods, you just didn't notice my legs were shaking. Besides, I had nothing to lose."

"What do you mean, Weza?"

"Just what I said. I had nothing to lose. I was sold because I am growing old, and I won't be able to do heavy work much longer. As I told you before, I wouldn't have lasted in the cotton fields. And all my family is dead and gone. You're different. Your mama is still alive in Winchester, and someday you'll see her again."

"I'm sorry, Weza. You've never mentioned your family. I thought you didn't have any."

"Everybody has someone sometime, child. Even your teacher."

"I doubt that. At least you had Otis, but she's an old maid, and she'll stay an old maid. Who could ever like anybody so pale and shriveled up?"

"You might be surprised," Weza said. "I've thought about it, and I'm convinced that you should ask her help."

"She won't help me," Lottie said.

"Your Miss Bosworth came all the way from Massachusetts to teach. Do you really think she will refuse to help someone who wants to learn?" Weza knelt over her washtub again and began scrubbing a nightshirt as she spoke. "Have you thought how difficult it is for her? I don't think any of those American Missionary Association folks had any idea of what they would find here. Most of them, like Miss Bosworth, even brought all the wrong clothes. She must just about die in her wool dresses. Springtime in Virginia must be a lot warmer than springtime in the North."

Lottie looked down at her feet and wriggled her toes in the dust. "I'll try to ask her," she said, wondering if Weza knew how difficult it would be.

Several days went by before Lottie got up the courage to stay after school. Miss Bosworth was packing up the materials she had used that day and didn't immediately notice Lottie. When she looked up over her glasses and saw Lottie standing by her desk, she said, "Yes, Lottie, may I help you?" Lottie lingered for a second before bolting for the door.

That night at dinner, Lottie looked down at her tin plate and told Weza. "I tried to talk to Miss Bosworth, today."

"And...," Weza said, expectantly.

"I couldn't ask her," said Lottie.

"I've had an idea," Weza began, hesitantly. When the days had gone by and there had been no resolution to Lottie's problems at school, Weza had thought it all over again, and she had been waiting for the right moment. "Why don't you ask Miss Bosworth to help you write a letter to your mama?"

Lottie looked up suddenly. "Write to Mama?" she said uncertainly. "Mama can't read."

"I know she can't," Weza said. "But she could find someone to read it to her. She would know you were safe if she got a letter. She'd know where to find you when this war is over."

"Oh, Weza, do you really think I could?"

"I know you can...if Miss Bosworth will help."

The next day, Lottie got up the courage to ask Miss Bosworth for help. Weza was right again. "Why, I'd be glad to give you extra help, Lottie," Miss Bosworth said when she had heard Lottie's sad story of slavery and separation. "My mother recently died, and I know firsthand how difficult it is to lose someone you love. We'll begin tomorrow after school."

Chapter 17
Dirty, Ragged Nails

A teacher with contraband children

From Lewis C. J. Lockwood, *Mary S. Peake, The Colored Teacher at Fortress Monroe* (Boston: American Tract Society, 1863).

"Try to read this," Miss Bosworth told Lottie as they sat together in the shade of a large oak. Lottie looked at the words; they seemed to swim before her eyes. The teacher had been working with her every day for a week now. But so far, Lottie was making little progress. A squirrel watched them from a branch above, then scampered off.

Lottie took a deep breath. "Could you please spell the words for me?" she asked.

Miss Bosworth patiently began reading the letters, "T-h-e o-l-d m-a-n."

"The old man," Lottie said without a pause.

Miss Bosworth looked at her, unsure what was going on. She read more letters, " w-e-n-t t-o t-h-e s-t-o-r-e."

"Went to the store," Lottie said.

Miss Bosworth was confused. She was not an experienced teacher. Along with the other missionaries, she had some instruction before coming south, but it had not prepared her for the reality of teaching children, children who had no exposure to reading, writing, and arithmetic. She still had not totally adjusted to the conditions at Fortress Monroe, the crowding in the shanty towns, the dirt, the wretchedness of the former slaves. Her long skirts were either dragging in the muddy streets or dingy from their yellow dust. It was a struggle just to keep clean. And now she didn't understand how Lottie was able to understand the words when they were spelled out for her.

A group of soldiers rode by, their uniform buttons and sword hilts glittering in the afternoon sunshine. Miss Bosworth's glasses reflected the glare from their shining brass. Suddenly, she had an idea. Maybe Lottie wasn't as slow a learner as she appeared. Taking off her glasses, she handed them to Lottie, "Here, put these on," she said.

From the tone of the teacher's voice, Lottie knew she had to do what Miss Bosworth said. She carefully took the strange spectacles, hooked the wires over her ears, and looked up at Miss Bosworth. For the first time she saw the little lines around the soft brown eyes and the anxious expression in them. She turned to look at the tree, the rough bark seemed to leap out at her, and she saw a tiny red ant scurrying up the trunk. Amazed, she looked down at her hands. She saw them clearly for the first time. Her nails were ragged and dirty. She felt her face flame. She was so ashamed she quickly hid the offending hands, sticking them under her skirt.

"Here," Miss Bosworth said, "try reading these words."

Lottie looked down at the book her teacher held. The letters no longer swam before her eyes. She saw the letters she had memorized from the large posters in the front of the classroom form into words. She cautiously began to sound them out, repeating the letters to herself. "The apple tree is in the yard," she read.

Miss Bosworth began to laugh. "I should have known," she said, clapping her hands together. "You need glasses."

Lottie looked up at her teacher through the unaccustomed lenses. She saw no cause for rejoicing. She had known for a long time that she wasn't seeing well. When she had sewn the new collar and cuffs for her brown dress, she had great trouble sewing small, neat stitches. However, she had not

LESSON XXXIX.

bought	pleas-ant	daugh-ter	ap-pear-ance
chalk	char-coal	learn-ing	ea-ger-ness
health	six-teen	al-though	in-ter-est-ing

PHILLIS WHEATLEY.

PHILLIS WHEATLEY, whose likeness is on this page, was brought to this country from Africa in the year 1761. She was then between seven and eight years old. She was bought by Mrs. John Wheatley, a Boston lady, who chose her from a crowd of robust negroes, although she looked feeble and slender, because of her modest appearance and pleasant face.

A page from a schoolbook designed for freed slaves

Freedman's Third Reader (Boston: The American Tract Society, 1866);
Published with permission of Princeton University Library

realized until now that she could not read because her eyesight was so poor. She removed the glasses and handed them to Miss Bosworth who seemed very pleased with herself.

"I have to go now," Lottie said, struggling to control her emotions. She ran off before Miss Bosworth could say anything else.

Lottie found Weza, bending over the small patch of ground that she had made into a kitchen garden. She had borrowed a hoe and was in the process of hoeing their four struggling rows of squash, cucumbers, beans, and corn. "Weza, I'll never learn to read; I'll never write Mama," she said, fighting back tears.

Weza put down the hoe and wiped her hands on her apron. "Come inside. Tell Weza all about it," she said.

When Weza knew what had happened, she said, "You won't have to go to school for the time being. Suffering comes often enough to our door without inviting it in. I'm sorry I didn't know about your eyes."

"You don't need to be sorry, you had no way of knowing," Lottie said. She was glad that she wouldn't have to return to school or to the difficult lessons after school. Yet she felt a great sadness too, realizing that she would never write her mother a letter.

"Maybe if you help me more, we can save enough money to buy you glasses," suggested Weza, wondering how much such things cost. "One thing is for sure. When you wash clothes everyday, your nails will always be clean."

Chapter 18
Father Abraham

Weza and Lottie awoke when they heard several loud explosions in the distance. "What's happening?" Lottie asked, sitting up on the side of the loft where she slept on a pallet. "It sounds like another sea battle."

"It's cannon fire, a long way off," said Weza, getting up from the string bed in the corner of the room below. She pulled on a skirt over her shift. It was Sunday and the only day that Weza wasn't up before sunrise to begin her morning tasks.

"There's been a lot of soldiers around lately," said Lottie. "Do you suppose we're being attacked?"

"Maybe it has something to do with President Lincoln being here, if he's really here," Weza said. "Several former slaves swear they've seen him. But it may be only wishful thinking."

They heard a deep rumbling noise and another explosion. "Shall we go to the waterfront to see if there's a battle?" asked Lottie.

"No, let's have our breakfast and get ready for church. We'll go early. Someone there will know what's going on."

An hour later, Lottie and Weza picked their way through the muddy streets of Grand Contraband Camp to Lottie's

President Abraham Lincoln, Secretary of War Edwin Stanton, Secretary of the Treasury Salmon P. Chase, and Major General John E. Wool at Fortress Monroe before the invasion of Sewell's Point, Norfolk, Virginia, on May 7, 1862

A drawing by Jack Clifton; courtesy of the Casemate Museum, Fort Monroe

school where a minister from the American Missionary Association held Sunday-morning church services. The rain-washed May morning smelled fresh and clean to Lottie, like the laundry when she took it in from their clothesline. She dreaded the prospect of going inside for the two-hour service, especially this morning with the roar of cannon in the air.

Small groups of people were gathered in front of the school talking. Josephine stood near the door with her two little girls. Weza went over to her and asked, "Do you know what's going on?"

"We've attacked Sewell's Point," Josephine said, excitedly. "That's where the cannon fire is coming from. President Lincoln is here overseeing military operations, and he's scheduled to inspect the troops later this morning. One of the officers at Fortress Monroe told me that the president will ride through Grand Contraband Camp on his way to the military encampment."

"Will we be able to see him?" Lottie asked. Miss Bosworth had told them in class that President Lincoln might free the slaves. Lottie wondered if that meant she would be reunited with her mother.

"Everybody's going to line up along the main road after church. General Wool, the commandant at Fortress Monroe, will probably take the president along the most direct route through the camp," said Josephine. "Everyone says he'll probably travel up Lincoln Street, named in his honor."

As they were talking, the sexton came to the church door and rang a hand bell for the service to begin. They went inside, and the service began earlier than usual. Lottie was unable to to concentrate on what the minister was saying. All she could think about was that she might get a chance to see President Lincoln. There was a picture of him in her classroom. She often had studied the craggy face, thinking that although he looked stern, there was kindness in his expression. Now perhaps she would get a chance to see him. She stood to sing "A Mighty Fortress Is Our God" with the others.

Finally, the church service was over. Lottie and Weza went back outside. The day was warming up, and there were many freed slaves milling about, awaiting the appearance of President Lincoln and the official party.

Weza and Lottie stationed themselves along the road. There was an air of repressed excitement as everyone anxiously looked toward Fortress Monroe, hoping to see something. Time passed slowly. The crowd of freed slaves along the road grew. Lottie heard someone say, "Father Abraham is our savior." Someone else responded, "Amen." These words seemed to sum up the almost religious faith that the contraband slaves had in President Lincoln.

Noon came and passed. Lottie was hungry. She had been too excited to eat much breakfast. She regretted it now. She was not far from their shanty, and she could have gone back home to have something to eat, but she didn't want to lose her place along the road. Several children spontaneously sang a little song that Lottie had heard at recess:

> *Abe Lincoln is a gentleman*
> *Jeff Davis is a mule*
> *Abe Lincoln is a gentleman*
> *Jeff Davis a fool!*
>
> *Shout boys, shout*
> *for I am a Union man*
> *Oh Yankee doodle dandy*
> *Hurrah for Uncle Sam!*

Lottie didn't sing with the others. She was too filled with anticipation. Suddenly, there was a commotion coming from the direction of Fortress Monroe. Everyone seemed to be talking at once as they saw soldiers and men in top hats approaching on horseback. Lottie jumped up and down, unable to contain her enthusiasm. "It's him!" she shouted to Weza, trying to be heard above the clamor all about them. Many people began running in the direction of the approaching party. "Maybe we should go too." Lottie pointed to the throng of people going to meet the president.

"We better stay here," Weza cautioned. "He'll go right by us."

Lottie kept jumping up, trying to catch a glimpse of the president. But there were too many people assembled all along the way for her to see clearly. Finally, the entourage neared.

Everybody around Lottie began to cheer. Lottie recognized President Lincoln. He was the tallest member of the group. He looked huge, astride a great black horse. His face was gray and drawn in the harsh sunlight. He rode with his head slightly inclined, trying to listen to something the officer next to him was saying. Standing with Weza, Lottie was no more than six feet from the great man. Behind them eager spectators pushed and shoved, trying to edge closer to the president.

Right in front of Lottie and Weza, the president's party halted. Lottie held her breath as Lincoln paused, took off his top hat, and waved it at the crowd along each side of the road. As he did so, a roar went up from the freedmen and women and for just a fraction of a second the president's shadow fell across Lottie. Her heart leapt. She looked up into his face and saw reflected there her sadness and that of all her people. He looked like his picture, but there was a difference. His rough features seemed to be worn down, like old saddle leather.

The moment passed, and the president continued on his way. "I'll never forget this day as long as I live," Lottie said, turning to Weza. Tears were streaming down Weza's face. In all they had been through, Weza had never cried. Now joy touched her in a way that sorrow never could. She smiled through her tears and dabbed at her eyes with a handkerchief. Lottie hugged Weza, and for a few seconds they savored the elation they both felt.

"Glory hallelujah," said Weza and her words sounded like a prayer.

Chapter 19

A World of Detail

Lottie delivered the last basket of clothes. It was a warm day and carrying the heavy baskets of laundry had tired her. She walked to her favorite spot, a tree stump near a bend in the north-south road. Putting down her basket, she sat on the stump. She watched the stream of refugees coming into Grand Contraband Camp, searching each face. President Lincoln's visit had renewed the hope that she would be re-united with her mother, and since she was no longer in school, she often had time to come here. Clouds of dust signaled the approach of a heavily laden wagon. A squad of soldiers, heading north moved aside so that the vehicle could pass. It lumbered by Lottie, creaking and rumbling on the rough road.

After it passed, she heard someone say, "There's Lottie." She turned to see a girl and two boys, coming from school.

"Lot-tie, dum-my," one called out. It was Phoebe, walking with her brother Rafe and his friend Sag. Rafe was older than Phoebe, and Lottie thought he was just as mean. Phoebe sang out again, "Lot-tie, dum-my. One and one is two, that's all Lottie can do."

Angry and hurt, Lottie jumped down from the stump, grabbed her basket, and ran. "Lot-tie, dum-my. Lottie dum-my," she heard behind her.

She raced up Lincoln Street, fleeing their taunts. She ran all the way to the shanty, and as she neared it, she looked around for Weza. Her washtub stood propped up by the side of the shanty and laundry flapped on the line. But Weza was nowhere in sight.

"Weza?" she called, going inside.

Weza was sitting at the table in the center of the room, and she was not alone. Miss Bosworth was sitting in their only chair. Lottie bit her lip, and then struggling to remember her manners, said, "Good afternoon, Miss Bosworth."

"Hello, Lottie," the teacher said with a warm smile. "We've missed you at school."

Lottie's first thought was that the teacher had come to make her go back to school, to make her go back, even though she couldn't learn.

"I have something for you, from the Missionary Association." The teacher handed Lottie a little box. "Go ahead, open it," she said.

Lottie carefully opened the lid. Inside was a pair of glasses, just her size.

"Try them on," Miss Bosworth said. "They're for reading. Now you can come back to school."

Without a word, Lottie put on the glasses. Weza laughed. "You look like a teacher," she said. "Now someday you'll be able to write that letter to your mama."

"Thank you, Miss Bosworth," Lottie said, a world of detail swirling before her eyes as she turned her head. "Thank you! Thank you!"

"I'll expect you in class tomorrow," said Miss Bosworth, standing to leave. "I'm so happy to have met you, Weza, and I'm glad we had a chance to talk." She took Weza's hand and shook it formally.

Weza smiled broadly, "Do come and see us again," she said, as she walked with Miss Bosworth to the door.

After Miss Bosworth left, Lottie slowly and carefully looked around. She noted the grain in the rough boards that made up their table, as intricate as the lines in her own palm. She hastily checked her nails, now clean and neatly clipped. She went to the shelves by the fireplace and carefully examined their metal mess kits, marveling at the tiny, hairlike scratches made by their knives and forks. She took down the brown paper packet, filled with the salt. She poured some tiny grains onto her hand and looked at them intently. She did the same with the cornmeal and the flour.

"You never knew what you were missing, is my guess," said Weza, enjoying Lottie's obvious delight.

Lottie turned to look at her friend, seeing Weza's careworn face clearly for the first time. "I never knew your face was so...," she paused, looking for the right word, "so beautiful," she said.

"Oh, go on," said Weza with embarrassment. "I'm an old woman." They both laughed and shared a hug.

Chapter 20
Lottie's Letter

One wintery day, Lottie arrived home from school at the usual time. It was the first sunny day for weeks, and Weza was hanging out a huge wash. Lottie put on an apron over her coat and went to help. She took several towels out of the clothes basket and began hanging them up.

"How was...," Weza stopped talking in midsentence.

Lottie turned to look at her. Her mouth fell open. She stood and stared. In front of Weza stood a man with skin as dark as her own. He was a handsome young man, tall and well built, and he wore the blue uniform of the Union army.

Weza asked, "May I help you, sir?"

"Yes," the soldier said. "I'd like my laundry washed." The man either was unaware of the shock he had caused or he had grown used to people staring at him.

"You've come to the right place," Weza said. And then, she didn't know what else to say. She knew the army was recruiting former slaves, but this was the first time she had seen one all decked out in the official uniform of the U.S. Army.

Weza found her voice and a few minutes later had arranged to do the man's laundry. When the soldier left, Lottie said, "I've never felt so proud as I did when I realized that man was wearing the same uniform as the men who saved us from the slavers."

"I know," Weza said, "I know just how you feel. To see him standing there in the prime of his life in that blue uniform sent shivers down my spine. I was just about to ask about your day when I saw him. How did school go today?"

"Miss Bosworth thinks I'm ready to write to Mama. She even gave me two pieces of her own paper. She calls it stationery," said Lottie.

Later that evening, Lottie sat down at the table after supper to write to her mother. A fire crackled in the fireplace, and a pitch pine knot burned in a saucer, casting a flickering light on the paper. She had placed her doll, her tow bag, and what was left of the pink cloth on the table. She was finding it difficult to put words to paper, and she hoped that the things that most reminded her of Mama would help her find the right words. As she thought, she absentmindedly fingered the material from time to time.

"What's the matter, honey?" Weza asked after a while. "You're not writing."

"I've worked hard for months and months learning to write, but now that I know how, I don't know what to say. I want to tell Mama everything, but that would take more than these two pages of stationery. It's impossible to put all my love in a short letter."

"Do the best you can," Weza said, deep in thought. She had never written nor received a letter, and she didn't know how to tell Lottie to proceed. "Your mama will like whatever you say."

Lottie bent over the paper and slowly began to print the letters. The fire had burned low, and it was almost bedtime when she sat up. "I've finished it," she said, holding out the letter for Weza to see.

"Why, that's wonderful," said Weza, admiring the neat lines of words.

"I think it's ready to send. Miss Bosworth is going to read it over for me tomorrow and help me address the envelope. I'm glad I've finally gotten the letter written, but I'm still worried because Mama can't read. I wish there was some way she'd know it was from me."

"Think about it, overnight," said Weza. "Maybe you'll come up with something. In the meantime, tell me what you wrote to your mama."

"I'll read it to you."

December 18, 1862

Dear Mama,

I am free now and at Grand Contraband Camp near Fortress Monroe. Weza is my friend. She looks after me. We escaped from the slavers. I go to school and help Weza do laundry.

I will stay here so you can find me when the war is over. Miss Bosworth is my teacher. She said that is the best plan.

We are well and hope you are the same. I miss you all the time. I cannot wait until we are together again.
I love you,
Lottie

"That's a mighty fine letter," said Weza.

"Writing is hard. Miss Bosworth has been a big help. Phoebe calls me teacher's pet every time she sees me," Lottie said.

"Phoebe's just jealous."

"Why would anyone be jealous of me?" asked Lottie.

"Phoebe is homely, and you aren't," said Weza. "Handsome is as handsome does. You have a nice way about you. You're not loud or ugly acting like some children."

Lottie was unaccustomed to compliments. She wasn't sure how to respond. After a moment, she said, "I've always hated being shy. I never thought that it was better than being loud."

"You're not as shy as you used to be," said Weza with satisfaction.

Lottie didn't know what else to say, so she turned the conversation back to her letter. "When do you suppose Mama will get this?" she asked, as she folded it neatly before putting it on the table.

"It may take a long time because of the war," said Weza thoughtfully. She dared not mention that in these unsettled times Lottie's mother might not get the letter at all. Weza patted Lottie's shoulder. "Then again, she may get it sometime soon."

Chapter 21
Under the Emancipation Oak

"May I ask a question?" Lottie asked Miss Bosworth one cold day after school when she was helping her teacher make badges for the field day that was to be held tomorrow.

"Of course," said Miss Bosworth. She finished sewing a rosette and handed it to Lottie who tied a white ribbon on it. Miss Bosworth stretched her cramped fingers. "I've told you repeatedly that you *must* ask questions when you don't understand something. Otherwise, you'll never learn."

"I don't understand all the fuss about reading the Emancipation Proclamation," Lottie said.

"Do you understand what the word emancipation means?" Miss Bosworth asked, picking up another swatch of material.

"I think so," Lottie said. "It means we're free." She hesitated and continued. "But I thought we were free as soon as we got here. Everybody calls this place Fortress Freedom and us freedmen and freedwomen. And we're treated like we're already free."

"I understand your confusion, Lottie," Miss Bosworth said. "Contraband slaves are a special case, and in fact contraband status has come to mean freedom for escaped slaves.

The proclamation refers to slaves in the Southern states. Last September, President Lincoln issued an order that does not go into effect until tomorrow. Before his order—the proclamation—the status of slaves in the South was uncertain. The proclamation frees the slaves in the Confederate states."

"Why are we celebrating it if we are already free?" Lottie asked.

"President Lincoln hopes that the proclamation will prevent European countries from supporting the Confederate cause and that it will encourage slaves to rebel throughout the South."

"Is that all?" Lottie asked.

"No," Miss Bosworth said. "Abolitionists in the North—people like me—have long hoped and worked to achieve an end to slavery. We see this as an important step toward that goal."

"I *see* now," Lottie said with an impish smile. She liked to use the word "see" when talking with Miss Bosworth.

"Can you *see* your way clear to pass me the scissors?" asked her teacher with a smile. "We'll finish this batch and then put everything away. It's getting late."

Lottie helped Miss Bosworth with the last rosettes. Lottie was sure that her school would have the nicest badges at the field day tomorrow. She carefully put them into a box to take to the celebration. Miss Bosworth locked the extra red material and white ribbon in the cupboard in the classroom. She handed Lottie her rosette as they headed out the door. "You may take this home to show Weza," she said. "Are you taking part in the events tomorrow?"

"Weza wants me to," Lottie said, looking down at the worn granite front steps. "So, I guess I will."

"I'll look for you, then," said Miss Bosworth with a goodbye wave of her hand.

Back at the shanty, Josephine was visiting Weza. "Where's Lottie?" Josephine asked.

"She's helping her teacher get ready for the celebration tomorrow. She's due back anytime now. That girl still worries me. She isn't through grieving for her mama, and she's grown attached to her teacher. The day will come for Miss Bosworth to go home to Massachusetts. I hate to have Lottie hurt again."

"She'll be all right as long as you're looking out for her," said Josephine.

They heard the door latch. "That'll be Lottie now," said Weza.

The following day, January 1, 1863, dawned bright and clear. Weza rose at sunup, but this morning she didn't do any washing. After breakfast, she bustled around and made a blackstrap molasses cake. She had converted the heavy iron skillet into an oven with the addition of a piece of metal she had scrounged. While she struggled with her makeshift oven, Lottie washed the breakfast dishes.

"Do you realize it is exactly one year to the day since we were sold in Williamsburg?" Weza asked as she took the cake out of the pan.

Lottie finished her chores and put on her brown coat, the same coat that Mama had found for her a year ago. "It's been a year since I've seen Mama," said Lottie, biting her bottom lip. "A whole year." She pinned the rosette on her coat. "I wish you had a rosette, too, Weza."

"I'm too old to wear doodads," said Weza, settling the matter in her usual no-nonsense manner. "And I wish you wouldn't wear your glasses to the field day. If you leave them here, you won't have to worry about them when you take part in the events."

"I don't want to take part," Lottie said.

"You're hiding behind those glasses," said Weza. "They're for school and sewing."

"I like to be able to see," said Lottie in a calm, respectful voice. She didn't want to be difficult, but she wanted to wear her glasses. Weza continually had stressed to Lottie that in dealing with customers, she should be firm, but pleasant. Now without thinking about it, Lottie had used the same technique with Weza.

Weza smiled and didn't say anything. She realized that Lottie's glasses enabled her to have a little control over her world, and she was pleased with how Lottie had handled the situation.

Weza wrapped the cake in brown paper. When she was done, they were ready to go to the live oak where the ceremony was to be held.

They arrived at the old oak early, but so did many others. Freed slaves and off-duty soldiers in their blue uniforms stood side by side in the pale yellow, morning sunshine, waiting for the festivities to begin.

Emancipation Oak on the campus of Hampton University, Hampton, Virginia
Courtesy of Alexander H. Haislip

With its wide canopy, the tree was an ideal spot to hold the important ceremony. In the warmer months when the crowded classrooms were hot, teachers sometimes taught classes under it. The oak was one place everyone in the area knew, and as a result, it was a favorite meeting place, especially on steamy summer days. Then its spreading branches offered a shady respite from the blazing Virginia sun.

This morning in the bright January sunshine, a wooden platform stood beneath it. On the platform were five chairs. Two well-dressed white men in black suits and stovepipe hats were seated there already. A third man, a distinguished-looking, white-haired African American in a top hat was talking to some of the freed slaves.

Lottie waited with Weza for the celebration to begin. All around her, the crowd continued to grow. There were thousands of inhabitants at Fortress Freedom now, and as Lottie looked about, she was sure that almost everyone had turned out for this occasion.

Finally, from the direction of Fortress Monroe came the rattle of drums and then the stirring sound of a band playing the tune, "When Johnny Comes Marching Home." As the band and a troop of soldiers drew near, Lottie saw the white-haired man join the dignitaries on the platform. Several important-looking army officers arrived at the oak with an escort of troops. Two officers joined the men on the platform. The band played "Hail Columbia."

Lottie noticed two boys watching her. The shorter one, Sag, nudged Phoebe's brother Rafe. He joined his forefingers and thumbs and made a pair of glasses with his fingers. Rafe held them up to his eyes while Sag laughed and pointed at Lottie. She turned away, her cheeks flaming. The African American man was speaking now, but Lottie couldn't concentrate on what he was saying. She was dreading the school field day that would follow the ceremony.

After the preliminary speeches, the great moment came. One of the officers read the Emancipation Proclamation. It wasn't very long, and it seemed to Lottie that it had only taken a minute to read. There was a momentary pause when the officer finished. Then everyone burst into loud cheers. Hats flew into the air, and Weza turned and gave Lottie a bear hug. The tumult only died down when the band began playing "The

Battle Hymn of the Republic." Lottie had learned the words to the song in school, and now she sang along.

When the ceremony was over, Lottie went to an open area where the events were beginning, and Weza joined the women setting up the picnic dinner. She put her cake on a long plank table and joined Josephine who was helping two women start a campfire. With so much laundry to wash, Weza didn't get much time to visit. She was looking forward to catching up on the latest gossip.

Chapter 22

Little Miss Four Eyes

Lottie walked about for five minutes before finding her classmates under the red-and-white banner that Miss Bosworth had made to represent their school. Yesterday, the children chose teams for the different events. Lottie had not been picked for any of the teams, but the one-hundred-yard dash, the three-mile run, and the tug of war were open to everyone.

Activities started off with a one-legged relay race. Lottie watched as a teacher, the thin, sick-looking man she had seen the first day of school, tied two of her classmates' legs together with strips of burlap. The boys tried to walk and fell down. Everyone laughed. Lottie was glad she wasn't in this race.

When the six teams were ready, a judge blew a whistle, and the race began. Lottie rooted for her school. In spite of her reluctance to take part in the events, she became caught up in the excitement. Lottie jumped up and down when her team neared the finish line, only seconds behind the winning team, and she cheered when the judges awarded the red-and-white team a ribbon.

The second event was a sack race, and Lottie pushed her way through the crowd to be nearer to where the teacher

133

was tying a sack on a squirming boy from her school. Lottie looked around for Miss Bosworth. Instead of seeing her teacher, she met the mocking eyes of Rafe. He began to walk toward her. He was tall for his age and towered above the other children. Lottie turned abruptly and began walking in the other direction.

When she had gone a comfortable distance, she began circling back toward the sack race. She scanned the throng, hoping that she would not see Rafe. But as she looked behind her, she saw Rafe and his buddy, Sag. Her heart began to pound. She elbowed her way to where the sack race was beginning and stood beside several children from her school. She saw Miss Bosworth at the far end of the field, and she wondered if she should make her way there.

After the sack race, Lottie looked around. She didn't see her tormentors. Just to be safe, she thought she'd better stay with the others. The next event was the greased pig race. Lottie watched as six half-grown pigs were covered with bacon grease. The officials assigned a pig to each school. At the signal, the teachers would untie the pigs. The first team to catch a pig and bring it to the finish line would win.

A pistol shot started the race. The pigs, frightened by the crowd, the grease, and the pistol shot, took off in every direction. Crowds of children followed each pig. Everyone laughed when first one child and then another tried to catch and hold the slippery pigs. Lottie was swept along with the crowd, which divided into six groups as each followed a fleeing pig.

In the excitement of the chase, a big, heavy-set girl accidentally jostled Lottie. She stumbled and almost fell. Shaken, she stopped running with the others. She watched as the rest of the children sped after the pig. It was then she saw Sag and Rafe. They had stopped running with the others and were coming toward her.

"Let me see those glasses, Little Miss Four Eyes," Sag said. He had one broken tooth, and his eyes were close together. Lottie thought he looked like a rat. He showed his teeth as if he were about to eat her.

"No!" Lottie said, backing up. She turned and fled. The boys took off after her. Lottie tore through a group of people and up a side street, the two boys close behind. As soon as she entered the narrow side street with its ramshackle slab buildings, she knew it was a mistake. The street was deserted. Everyone who lived here was at the Emancipation Day celebration. Fear drove her forward until a sharp pain in her side caused her to slow her pace. When she slowed, Rafe overtook her.

"Where do you think you're going?" he asked as he roughly pushed Lottie to the ground. Sag grabbed her and held her down. Rafe snatched her glasses. Lottie watched in horror as he waved his prize above his head. Sag guffawed and let her go.

"Give me those!" Lottie cried, struggling up and lunging after the glasses.

"I want them," Rafe said, dodging Lottie and staying just out of her reach. "And I've got them." He put them on, prancing about and saying in a high voice, "I'm teacher's pet now. Can I help you, Miss *Bothers*-worth?"

"Let me see them," Sag said. Rafe took them off and tossed them to his friend.

Sag caught them with one hand. Lottie ran at him, but he scampered away. He had only gone a few feet when another boy slipped around the side of a shanty. He wore ragged clothes and a faded blue soldier's kepi. It was Ned from the tobacco barn. He didn't go to Lottie's school, and she rarely saw him. Whenever she did see him, Ned was always with a group. So she never spoke to him.

With a yell, he lunged at Sag and grabbed his arm, pinning it painfully behind him. "Give the glasses back!" Ned shouted, applying pressure to the boy's arm.

Seeing Sag was in trouble, Rafe took off in the direction of the celebration. Sag dropped the glasses. Lottie watched as they plummeted to the ground. He raised his foot to step on them, but before he could do it, Ned gave him a shove. Sag fell down with a cry. Lottie raced over and picked up her glasses. The frames were bent, and one lens had a tiny crack at the bottom of the glass. She put the glasses on before anything else could happen to them.

Lottie's protector wasn't through with Sag yet. Ned wasn't very tall, but he was sturdy and tough. He picked up Sag by the belt and hung him to a nearby fence. Lottie watched as Sag struggled in vain to free himself. She had to smile at the sight. Sag's belt was positioned so that he couldn't reach the buckle and he flailed around helplessly, trying to get free.

"You bother her again," said Ned, "and I'll get you and that other low-down rat too."

As they walked away, they heard Sag yell after them, "Don't leave me! Don't leave me! Get me down from here!"

"Thank you," Lottie said to Ned as they continued to walk away, ignoring Sag's pleas for help.

Ned grinned and his dark face lit up. "I was coming back to the celebration after running an errand for one of the officers when I saw those two chasing you. It made me mad to see two of them beating up on a girl."

"I'm glad you came along," Lottie said. "I can't attend school without my glasses." She peered through her glasses, and the hairline crack at the bottom of one lens seemed huge.

"You sound like you enjoy school," Ned said.

"I do," Lottie said. "Don't you?"

"Sometimes it's all right," said Ned. He took a blue-and-white badge from his pocket. "I'm at the old Tyler mansion. But I won't be there too much longer. As soon as I'm old enough, I'm going to get a job. I want to work for the army."

"Do you think they'll hire you?" Lottie asked, looking at Ned. She was finding it surprisingly easy to talk to him.

"I make a little money now, running errands," Ned said, his animated face growing suddenly serious. "And Mama needs it. We're just barely getting by."

It wasn't long before they arrived back at the field where the competitions were being held. The one-hundred-yard dash was just beginning. With so many people milling about, Lottie hoped she wouldn't run into Miss Bosworth. Lottie knew she would have some explaining to do, and she suddenly felt exhausted as if she had been running races all day long.

"Thanks again," Lottie said to Ned. "I have to find Weza. She'll be worrying about me."

Weza was sitting on a bench near where Lottie had left her, talking with a group of women. Lottie hesitated, dreading the moment when she would have to explain her damaged glasses.

Weza caught sight of Lottie, standing off to one side, and Weza sensed immediately something was wrong. "I'll be back," she told the others and hurried over to Lottie.

"What happened to you?" Weza asked, putting her arm around Lottie's shoulder and steering her away from the others.

"Boys chased me and took my glasses," Lottie said, biting her lip and swallowing hard. "Josephine's boy, Ned, drove them off."

Weza's brow was furrowed with concern. "Tell me all about it," she said.

After Lottie had told Weza the whole story, Weza asked, "Did they hurt you?"

Lottie shook her head. "I'm not hurt, but my glasses are cracked. What will Miss Bosworth say?"

"Don't you worry about that right now," Weza said. "I want you to promise that you'll never run away from anybody again."

"But," Lottie protested, "they were going to take my glasses."

"Glasses are only things. Things can be replaced. But if those boys had hurt you, that's another matter. It's dangerous to be caught in a deserted place. I want you to promise that in the future you'll stand your ground. We're no longer slaves. We're free now. If this celebration means anything, it means we don't have to run away anymore."

Lottie looked up at Weza. The older woman stood with her feet planted firmly on the ground and her hands on her hips. She was like an unmovable mountain, rugged and enduring. "I promise," Lottie said, hoping that she could live up to Weza's expectations and the promise she had just made.

Chapter 23
Miss Bosworth's Plan

Miss Bosworth didn't find out about the glasses until the next morning. Lottie went to school early to tell her teacher what had happened. "I'm not angry with you, Lottie," Miss Bosworth assured her. "But I want you to tell me in great detail everything that happened."

Lottie told Miss Bosworth about the incident with Rafe and Sag at the Emancipation Day celebration. When she was finished, Lottie asked, "Why are some of the children so mean to me?"

"I've heard people say that slavery is so evil that it has ruined your people," said Miss Bosworth. "But I don't believe it."

"I don't either," Lottie said. "Weza was a slave for a whole lot longer than Sag or Rafe, and it didn't make her mean."

Miss Bosworth thought for a few minutes. Since she had been teaching the contraband slaves, she had seen examples of courage and cowardice, honesty and deceit, kindness and cruelty. "Slavery is evil," she said. "And it has made dignity and honor difficult, often impossible, for some slaves. Yet others, like your friend Weza, have not let slavery destroy what is good in them. You must strive always to be like her."

"Were children ever mean to you when you were growing up?" Lottie asked.

Miss Bosworth smiled. "There are good and bad people everywhere, even in Massachusetts," she said. "There was a boy in my neighborhood who was always threatening to wash my face in a snowbank. He never did. But he was fond of pelting me with snowballs. Sometimes he put ice in the center of his snowballs, and it really hurt."

Just then, the bell rang for school to start. Miss Bosworth began her day concerned about Lottie. As more and more freed slaves had congregated around Fortress Freedom, the populace had become more and more unruly. The boys were a special problem. She knew full well the difficulty of trying to teach the boys who found their way here. Rafe and Sag were not bad boys, but they were out of control and potentially dangerous. She feared they would cause trouble for Lottie later on. She resolved to speak with Weza at the earliest possible moment.

The following week, Miss Bosworth found the opportunity. She knew Lottie delivered laundry on Saturday, and she found Weza home alone, ironing shirts she had washed the day before.

"Won't you come in and have a cup of mint tea?" Weza asked, when Miss Bosworth came to the door.

"Thank you, that would be nice," Miss Bosworth said, untying the strings of her bonnet and taking it off before placing it on the bench near the table.

When the tea was ready, Weza poured them both a cup and sat down at the table across from Miss Bosworth. Ever since the incident with the glasses, Weza had been expecting a visit from Lottie's teacher.

Miss Bosworth took a sip from the steaming cup. Now that she was here, she wasn't quite sure where to begin. Finally, she plunged in. "I've been concerned about Lottie. This place seems to grow wilder by the day. Just yesterday a delivery boy working for the army was beaten up and his money stolen."

"I know," Weza said. "I keep telling Lottie to be on her guard, to see trouble coming and get out of its way."

"You have done well by Lottie. I don't know what she would have done without you. I'm convinced that you want only the best for her."

"She's like a daughter to me," Weza said, wondering where all this was going.

"You may have heard," said Miss Bosworth, pausing to take another sip of the fragrant tea, "that there are several plans afoot to send young women and children north. The idea is that they will be found suitable places as domestic servants, with pay of course."

"I've heard about something like that," Weza said, looking intently at Miss Bosworth. The proposed plans to send some freed slaves north had been one of the things that she had discussed with the other women at the Emancipation Day celebration.

"Of course, I would never suggest such a thing for Lottie," Miss Bosworth spoke quickly now. "Lottie's a good student. She shows promise. Friends of the American Missionary Association are offering a scholarship to train future teachers at Miss Hinkley's Academy in Boston. The girl selected for the scholarship would receive free tuition and only have to work for her room and board."

Weza frowned at the prospect of Lottie leaving. "What kind of work would that be?" Weza asked without showing her feelings.

"The scholarship girls, both black and white, wait on tables in the dining room, help with sewing, and work in the laundry."

"How long would this schooling take?"

"It's hard to say exactly. But I'll be returning to Boston soon. And I'd be available if Lottie had any problems adjusting to the school."

"It sounds like a wonderful opportunity," Weza said, trying to sound enthusiastic. "But it'll be up to her. I'm no kin to her. She's her own person."

"I understand that Lottie isn't related to you. But I also know she trusts you. She'll do whatever you say."

Weza gave a sad little laugh. "What you say is true. But I wish it wasn't so. She needs to stand on her own feet. I won't always be here to shore her up."

The teacher stood and put on her bonnet. "Thank you for the tea. Think over my proposition," she said, extending a hand to Weza at the door. "We have some time yet before any decisions have to be made."

"I'll mull it over," Weza promised. She stood at the door for a long time, watching the slim figure of the teacher as she made her way up the rutted street in the direction of the school. Weza wanted what was best for Lottie. Miss Bosworth had been right about that. The only problem was Weza didn't know what that was.

Chapter 24

From the Heart

Clara Shadwell coughed and coughed. "You should do something about that," Henrietta said. "Ever since the weather turned cold, you've had an ugly cough."

"It seems I just can't shake it," said Clara.

"Go to bed. I'll talk to the missus."

Clara reluctantly went to her quarters. She hadn't been strong since she got sick last year. Now the sickness came over her in waves. First she felt hot, and then she felt cold.

Later, Henrietta came to see her. One look told Henrietta all she needed to know. "I'm afraid you've got pneumonia again," she said. "This time I'll try to get the missus to send for the herb woman right away."

Not long after Clara had taken to her bed, a redheaded boy was shown into the drawing room where Mr. Howell and Mrs. Howell sat having their morning coffee. Mr. Howell was a tall, broad-shouldered man. He shifted his position in the uncomfortable wing chair, and looking up from his newspaper, he asked, "May I help you?"

"I have a letter for a Mrs. Clara Shadwell," the boy said, standing at the edge of the India carpet.

"We've no one here with that name," said Mrs. Howell, annoyed by the interruption. A boy with a letter should have been dealt with at the back door.

"What about the cook?" asked her husband. "That's her name, I think, even though we call all our people 'Howell' here."

"That woman," Mrs. Howell said, "she's still in bed most of the time. I'm not sure that she isn't going to up and die on us."

Mr. Howell stood and dug in his pocket for a copper to give the boy. "Thank you," he said, taking the letter and giving it to his wife.

"The Negroes are more bother than they are worth," Mrs. Howell said after the boy had left. "We'll be lucky if we don't end up with an invalid on our hands."

Mrs. Howell began to open the letter. "Emma," her husband said sharply, "let the poor thing open her own letter."

"I'm sure she can't read," said Mrs. Howell defensively.

"That is not our concern," Mr. Howell said firmly. "With the war on, we've got more important things to worry about than a slave getting a letter."

Later that evening, Mrs. Howell gave Henrietta the letter. When her work was done, she took the letter to Clara, who lay in bed coughing. When the other slaves heard about the letter and saw Henrietta go to Clara's quarters, they came to the door. No slave at the Howell household had ever gotten a letter. It was cause for great excitement.

Clara couldn't believe there was a letter for her. She had never gotten a letter. When Henrietta gave it to her, she just held it in her hand. The letter must have passed through many hands because the envelope was dog-eared and dirty.

"Open it," Henrietta urged.

"I can't read," Clara said sorrowfully.

"Open it anyway," Henrietta said. "As soon as you're better, we'll find someone to read it. There's a freedman who works at the livery stable in Winchester who can read. I'm sure he'll read it for you."

With shaking hands, Clara opened the letter. The slaves looked on, breathless with excitement. There were two sheets of paper in the envelope. Clara took them out carefully and stared at them. Then she noticed something else in the envelope. Her long, thin fingers reached in and pulled out a small piece of fabric. The only light in the room was from the fireplace, and it took Clara a moment to realize what she was looking at. The material was sewn into the shape of a heart, and the heart was made of the material Major Shadwell had given her for Christmas before she left Williamsburg.

Clara started to cry. It was a letter from Lottie. Her little girl was alive and well and had written her a letter. She handed the heart to Henrietta. "From Lottie," she said through her tears. Henrietta passed the heart to the others. Each one looked at it silently, then looked at Clara. She was both smiling and crying.

The very next day Henrietta noticed a change in Clara. "My, my," she said, "you are looking better."

"I not only look better," Clara said, "I'm feeling stronger. I'm going to get well."

Henrietta smiled. "You just do that. And I'll go with you to the livery stable. I want to hear what your little girl has to say."

Chapter 25

Finding Friends

Months passed, and Miss Bosworth did not speak to Weza again about the possibility of Lottie attending school in Boston. After Ned rescued Lottie, they became friends. "I thought you didn't like me," Ned confessed to her one rainy spring day when he walked her home after school.

"Oh, no!" said Lottie, surprised and shocked that he should think such a thing.

"Well, you sure gave that impression," said Ned, teasing her just a little.

Lottie's face flushed. "Weza says I'm too shy and quiet sometimes. But she also says I'm getting over it."

Their conversation was interrupted by the appearance of an ambulance wagon. They moved out of the muddy roadway to let it rumble past. "A lot of people have come down sick," Ned said, shaking his head.

"I don't mind seeing the ambulance wagons," Lottie said. "It's the other wagons I don't like, the ones that take coffins to the cemeteries. If someone's in the hospital, I know that at least there's hope. With so much sickness about, I worry about my mother. She was often sick when we lived with Major and Mrs. Shadwell in Williamsburg. She got a lot of colds and fevers."

Ned didn't know what to say to reassure Lottie. With the overcrowding and bad weather, there had been fevers, poxes, and pneumonia throughout Grand Contraband Camp during the last few months. The soldiers in the various encampments around Fortress Monroe also fell ill with a variety of complaints. Ned decided not to say anything. Instead, he bounded forward and executed two perfect cartwheels in the narrow grassy space between the ruts made by wagon wheels.

Distracted by Ned's antics, Lottie clapped her hands approvingly. Ned seemed to have a knack for making her feel better.

They neared the shanty Lottie shared with Weza. "I gotta go," Lottie said. "Weza needs my help. Her business is booming."

Weza was just hanging up sheets when she spotted them. "Come over here, Ned," she called.

"What can I do for you, Miss Weza?" Ned asked with a big grin.

"I've got so much work to do with sickness everywhere, I just can't handle it all. I've ordered another washtub and scrub board from Amos Meyer. I should have it next week. Do you suppose your mama could help me out some?"

"I think she'd be pleased to," Ned said, knowing his mother, like the other women in camp, would be grateful for any work.

"Well, I'd like you to ask her to come by and see me tomorrow," said Weza.

The next morning Josephine came to their shanty early. "I want to work," she told Weza, "but I can't leave my girls."

"You can bring the girls along. I like to have children around. Let's try it."

"I'll come as soon as you get the washtub," said Josephine. Her round face glowed with anticipation. She would work hard so that Weza would keep her on.

Once Josephine was helping Weza, Ned came by more often. "Can Lottie come with me Sunday afternoon?" he asked Weza. "There's going to be a baseball game in the field near Emancipation Oak."

"Ask Lottie."

"What about it, Lottie?" he asked. "Some of the soldiers are playing. We'll just watch."

"I'd like that," said Lottie, thinking how much she enjoyed doing things with Ned. He always seemed to find a pleasant way to pass the free time she had on Sunday afternoons.

The following Sunday was warm and the heavy, sweet smell of magnolia blossoms filled the air. Lottie was ready when Ned came by the house. Weza watched them go off toward the ballfield. Lottie seemed at ease with Ned, and Weza was grateful that Lottie had a friend. Somehow her quiet ways balanced his cheerful, outgoing nature.

When May Day came, it rained in torrents, totally ruining plans at school for a Maypole. The children were so disappointed that the teachers arranged a taffy-pulling party. Lottie had never pulled taffy before. She stood with the others while Miss Bosworth lined them up in pairs, giving each pair a ball of taffy to pull. Lottie's partner was a new girl named Francine. Lottie had been watching Francine. She was a pretty girl with golden skin and deep dimples, but like Lottie, she appeared to be somewhat ill at ease with the other children.

Francine and Lottie began to stretch the taffy, both of them walking slowly backward. They stretched it and stretched it and stretched it. The taffy was sticky and difficult to manage, and they heard squeals of delight all around them. A lock of Lottie's hair came loose, and she reached up and brushed it away without thinking. The taffy stuck to her hair. Francine wrinkled her nose and began to giggle. When Lottie attempted to extract the taffy from her hair, it became tangled in her fingers. "I must look like a fly caught in a spider's web," she said and started to laugh. The tension she had felt pulling taffy with the new girl disappeared.

"I live in Slabtown, near the crossroads," said Francine hesitantly when they were cleaning up after the taffy pull. "I found a piece of rope the other day. It's just the thing for a jump rope. Maybe you could come over some afternoon, and we could jump rope."

"I deliver laundry after school," said Lottie. When she saw how disappointed Francine looked, she hastily added, "But I know where you live. Maybe on Saturday after I finish."

Francine smiled and nodded. "Our place is the shanty with the red roof."

"I don't know how to jump rope," said Lottie.

"It's easy. I'll show you," said Francine. She left with a wave and a smile. Lottie hurried home. She couldn't wait to tell Weza about the taffy pull and about Francine.

Chapter 26
He's Come for Us

The summer sun hung in the sky like a giant smoldering ember, and Lottie had spent the whole hot afternoon delivering laundry. She was hurrying to get done because she had promised Ned that she would go crabbing with him before dark. Her big delivery basket was almost empty, and her faded calico dress stuck to her skin as she walked slowly toward the center of Grand Contraband Camp. Occasionally, a slight breeze tugged at her straw hat.

She was looking for Mr. Meyer. She had some shirts and small clothes to return to him. Weza had been doing his laundry now for sixteen months. They had paid off all their debts to him, and now he was a customer, just like the others, although Weza gave him a reduced rate.

Even though the sutlers moved their wagons from place to place, Lottie had come to have a pretty good idea each week where she could find Mr. Meyer. He was the most dependable of the sutlers. This afternoon, she found his wagon in front of the new office for the Bureau of Negro Affairs.

At first, Lottie had been frightened of Mr. Meyer. He spoke sharply to everyone, and she had not known what to do when he tried to substitute damaged canned goods for the meager coins Weza charged him. Now, however, Lottie was used to dealing with Mr. Meyer, and she no longer was afraid of him. Today, she made the mistake of looking at the tomatoes that he had for sale. She wondered where Mr. Meyer had gotten them since he usually didn't sell produce.

"Here take these," he said, attempting to hand her three overripe and bruised tomatoes.

Lottie refused to take them. "The tomatoes are bruised. My money, please," she said, planting her feet firmly and holding out her hand.

"Little Miss," Mr. Meyer said, "you are becoming a good businesswoman, just like Miss Weza." He handed her a nickel, and she handed him his clean shirts and underwear.

"Here," Mr. Meyer said, not looking at her, "take a couple of these tomatoes, no charge."

"Thank you, Mr. Meyer," Lottie said, taking the tomatoes and putting them into the pocket of her apron. The old man had shown them many kindnesses, but he always refused to acknowledge them. Now he waved her away with a motion of his hand. Lottie picked up the basket and went off in the direction of her last delivery for the day.

As Lottie headed away from the sutler's wagon, she felt suddenly uneasy as if someone was staring at her. A tall, well-built man with blue-black skin in a new-looking suit stood in front of the Bureau of Negro Affairs. Lottie wondered if he was one of the new officials connected to the office. Beside him stood another man who was looking directly at her. His whisker-shrouded face was all but hidden by a slouch hat, but

Lottie would know him anywhere. It was the slave trader, Nephus Slye.

At the moment that Lottie made this discovery, she saw a flicker of recognition pass over the slave trader's face. Lottie felt a chill, as if someone had opened one of the long-deserted tombs in the churchyard of St. John's Church. Her pulse began to race. She wanted to drop her basket and run, but she was riveted to the spot. And she had promised Weza that she would never run away again.

Slye was engrossed in a discussion with the well-dressed man. Slowly, with a tremendous force of will, Lottie turned and walked back to Mr. Meyer's wagon. The sutler was waiting on a soldier. Lottie could feel her heart pounding, as if it were inside her head and trying to get out. She could feel Slye's one eye boring through her back.

When Amos Meyer finished, he came over to Lottie. "Yes," he said, peering down at her through his thick lenses. "Did you forget something, Little Miss?"

Lottie opened her mouth to speak and found she could not. She was seized again with an overwhelming urge to bolt.

The old man, long accustomed to the world and its ways, immediately recognized the terror on Lottie's face. "Come," he said, and placing a firm hand on her arm, he steered her around to the other side of his wagon where he had placed a chair in the shade. He had angled the chair so that he could see the road if any customers approached, but they couldn't see him. He motioned toward the chair. "Put your basket down, sit, and tell me the problem."

Lottie felt a little better once the firm chair was beneath her. She swallowed and bit her lip. It was a moment before she could speak. She took a deep breath. "That man over there," she began, pointing out Slye. "He's the slave trader who bought me. Weza and I escaped from him. Now he's here, talking with someone from the bureau. He's come for us!" Tears began to roll down Lottie's face. "I don't know what to do."

Amos Meyer didn't know what to do either. He didn't know anything about slave traders. Yet he had experienced fear like Lottie's. Until he came to America, he had lived in fear. His family had once owned a small dry goods store in Vienna, Austria, until vandals wrecked it one night and the police did nothing. Life was better here in Virginia, yet some people still hated him for his religion. They hated him without even knowing him. So for years, he had dealt gruffly with a world that had treated him unfairly. Now this little girl was doing her best not to cry. And in her suppressed tears he saw the tears of his mother and sisters and all the Jews driven from their homes and persecuted.

"I'm going to close my business. Stay here," he said, turning to the task of putting things away and closing down the sides of the wagon. He locked everything and then returned to where Lottie was sniffling and watching Slye.

"Wipe your eyes; we'll find Miss Weza," he said, handing Lottie one of the clean handkerchiefs she had just returned to him. He picked up her basket with one hand and put it under his arm. He put the other protectively around Lottie's shoulders.

Weza was on her knees weeding their garden when she saw the strange sight of Lottie coming up the lane with the sutler. She struggled to her feet and washed her hands in the water bucket that stood by their front door. After she heard what had happened, her face grew hard. "That man Slye is a snake," she said. "And you never know where he'll hide or when he'll strike."

"I think you're safe here with soldiers everywhere," said Mr. Meyer. "I haven't heard of the soldiers returning any runaway slaves. As I understand it, you're free now."

Weza thought about what Amos Meyer said for a minute. "The day we arrived we were warned that former slaves sometimes were kidnaped. There's nothing I'd put past Slye's kind of scum."

Amos Meyer nodded his head in agreement. He knew just what kind of person she was talking about. Some people broke the law, no matter what the consequences. And sometimes the law was blind as it had been in Vienna. "I don't know what to tell you," he said in a sad voice.

"Maybe Miss Bosworth would know what to do?" Lottie suggested.

Weza shook her head. "This is one situation that I don't think your teacher will understand, Lottie. People like her are protected by the laws. I'm not sure how much protection we can ask for and get. I need to think about it. Thank you,

Mr. Meyer, for bringing Lottie home. If you wait a minute, I have something for you."

"That's all right," Amos Meyer said as he began to walk away.

"Please wait here a minute," Weza said firmly, ignoring his eagerness to leave.

Weza went inside and returned a minute later. She carried something wrapped in a clean, checkered hand towel. "Two baked potatoes for your supper," she said, handing Amos Meyer the bundle. "They've been baking all day in the coals from this morning's fire." The old man nodded and took his leave. Lottie thought she saw just the trace of a smile on his narrow lips as he walked in the direction of his wagon.

Chapter 27

Decisions

Lottie and Weza ate their supper of butter beans, tomatoes, and leftover biscuits in silence, each deep in thought. They were just putting away their dishes when Ned came to the shanty to take Lottie crabbing.

"I'm sorry," Weza said. "Lottie can't go with you tonight. We'll explain later."

Ned looked disappointed. But he knew from the distressed tone of Weza's voice that it would be better if he came back another time. "I'll catch up with you later," said Ned agreeably.

"I need to talk to you," said Weza after Ned left. Weza told Lottie about the opportunity for her to study at a school in Boston. "I didn't tell you before," she said, "I thought I'd wait until it was more than just talk. I didn't want you to be disappointed if nothing came of it. But just yesterday, Miss Bosworth told me that the place was available for certain, and she needs to know by next week if you'd like to accept the scholarship. I think we ought to tell Miss Bosworth that you'd be willing to go to Boston."

Lottie took in everything Weza said. The chance to study in Boston and become a teacher was almost beyond Lottie's comprehension. She had heard rumors about sending a student to Massachusetts, but it had never occurred to her that she might be the one selected. Miss Bosworth had many good students, and it was an honor to be chosen. Lottie had heard people talk about "golden" opportunities. And she had never quite understood what that meant until now. She would love to be a teacher!

Her elation at the prospect, however, was short-lived. "I'd like to go, but I can't for two reasons," said Lottie. "When I wrote Mama, I told her I'd stay here until the war was over. She'll come here to find me. Miss Bosworth said that was a good plan."

"And what's the other reason?" Weza asked.

"I don't want to leave you," said Lottie. "I've lost Mama, and even though I hope and pray I'll see her again, I don't know if I ever will. I try not to think about that, but I know in my heart it's true. I can't lose you too."

"Why, you wouldn't lose me if you went away," Weza said, turning her head to hide the fact that she was near tears. "You could write me. Besides, there's no telling what that Slye is up to. I wouldn't trust him as far as I could throw him."

"Weza, you want me to run away," Lottie said in amazement. "You made me promise I'd never run away again. And today I didn't, even though I wanted to. Now you want me to leave Fortress Freedom because that low-down slaver might be up to no good."

Weza said, "I've thought about this Boston thing long and hard. If you care for someone, you want what is best for them. And I've thought it through, and I think you shouldn't pass up a once-in-a-lifetime opportunity like this."

"Then how come you haven't even mentioned it until today?" Lottie asked.

"I've been weighing things in my mind for a long time. Today, the scales tipped in favor of Boston. We don't know how the war will end. I heard that the South has invaded the North. Imagine that. A big battle started the day before yesterday up in a place called Gettysburg in Pennsylvania. If the South wins this war, we could all be slaves again. If you were in Boston, though, you'd be free forever."

"But Weza," Lottie protested, "the North may win the war soon and Mama may make her way here. What if she got here and couldn't find me?"

"I think you should go," Weza said. "But it's your decision, not mine or Miss Bosworth's. And you must make it and live with it."

"I'm going to stay here," Lottie said with a self-assuredness that was unusual for her. "And we need to decide what to do about Slye. What can we do?"

Weza looked relieved. "Are you sure, Lottie?"

"Yes, Weza, I've never been more sure of anything," said Lottie. She went over to the old woman who had become very dear to her and gave her a long hug.

"Well," said Weza, swallowing hard to overcome her emotions, "in that case, as soon as it's light tomorrow, I'm going to try and find the man you saw with Slye. We'll see if we can learn what that snake is up to. In the meantime, I want you to stay close. You'll have to miss school, and we'll deliver the laundry together."

It was Rastus who helped them out the next afternoon. "The well-dressed man is a Mr. Potter," he said, scratching his old mule behind the ears as they talked. "He's from Boston, a member of the Missionary Association."

"Do you know where I could find this Mr. Potter?" Weza asked.

"Sure do," said Rastus with a big smile. "He's staying over at the old Tyler mansion. I was by there yesterday."

Both Weza and Lottie had been to the large, white Tyler house. The building was used as a school and a temporary residence for several teachers from the American Missionary Association. As they approached it, Lottie recognized the well-dressed man she had seen yesterday. He was sitting on the porch with the Missionary Association minister. Lottie was glad that they didn't have to knock at the door and ask for him. She followed Weza up the path that led to the wide porch. "Could I speak to Mr. Potter, please?" Weza asked when they neared.

Mr. Potter stood. "I'll be a moment," he told the minister. He came down the front steps and stood beside Weza and Lottie.

"Roger Potter, ma'am," he said. "I don't believe I've had the pleasure of your acquaintance."

**Summer residence of ex-President John Tyler. It
was used as a school and to house members
of the American Missionary Association.**

Frank Leslie's *Illustrated Weekly,* August 10, 1861;
courtesy of the Casemate Museum, Fort Monroe

Weza introduced herself and Lottie and told him the
purpose of their visit. Mr. Potter listened to them carefully
and then laughed. "I don't know anyone named Slye. I know
the man you're talking about though. A one-eyed fellow with
dirty hair. He called himself Brown. He wanted to sell slaves,
said he knew where they were hid and some low-life that
wanted to sell them. I didn't know what to do. The American
Missionary Association has almost no money. Our resources
are stretched to the limit and beyond."

"So what happened to Slye?" Weza asked.

"I spoke to the representative of the Bureau of Negro
Affairs this morning, and he advised me to report him to General Butler at Fortress Monroe, which I did. Brown, or Slye

as you call him, was arrested for trying to sell slaves. I saw the soldiers arresting him myself."

"I feel sorry for the people he was trying to sell," Weza said.

"So do I, ma'am, but the Missionary Association can't afford to buy slaves, if he really would have delivered them. And besides, what he was trying to do is against the law in territories held by the United States government," said Mr. Potter, taking out his handkerchief and wiping the sweat from his brow. "I think he'll be in jail a good long time. After learning he was a slave trader, I'm more certain than ever that I did the right thing."

Weza and Lottie thanked Mr. Potter and walked back to their shanty. "Weza, I feel like I am walking five feet off the ground," said Lottie as they neared home.

"I know, I feel that way, too. When I heard Slye was here, it was like a dark cloud blotted out the sun. I didn't think he could get us now. But I wasn't sure. I guess we'll never be really sure about that one. But I like the idea of him behind bars. He'll learn firsthand how precious freedom is. I hope he'll be locked up for a long, long time."

"Tomorrow's July Fourth, and we have more reason than ever to celebrate," said Lottie.

When they got to the shanty, they found Ned sitting outside on an overturned washtub. He jumped up when he saw them. "General Lee is retreating from Gettysburg!" he said, barely containing his excitement. "And over in the west, Vicksburg is surrendering tomorrow!"

"Glory hallelujah!" said Weza. "The North is winning!"

"Can we take the day off and go to all the Fourth of July activities?" Lottie asked.

"I wouldn't miss a minute of it for the world," said Weza. She turned to Ned. "Why don't you come in, Ned, and we'll plan where to meet tomorrow."

Chapter 28

Locked Up

It was a sultry August afternoon in Winchester where Clara lived with the Howells. She had made blackberry tea yesterday, and it had been cooling in the springhouse since then. She put a big pitcher of tea on a tray with two glasses and carried it toward the veranda. Mr. and Mrs. Howell were sitting there to escape the afternoon heat.

Suddenly, Clara felt faint. She had been on her feet all morning, and since her bouts of sickness, she sometimes became lightheaded. Putting her tray down, she sat for a moment in a red damask-covered chair near a window that opened onto the veranda. She could not help but overhear Mr. and Mrs. Howell talking.

"I think we have no alternative. We should lock up the slaves at night," Mrs. Howell told her husband. "That's the only way we'll keep the few we've got left."

"Most of the ones who wanted to run off have gone already," Mr. Howell replied without looking up from his newspaper.

"Our Confederate army hasn't given us enough protection. We've lost nearly half of our people already, and I don't want to lose the rest," said Mrs. Howell in an irritable tone of voice. "That Clara is still sullen; she'd go if she could."

"Where's a crippled woman going to run to?" asked Mr. Howell with a resigned sigh. His wife had her good qualities, but she seemed to have it in for their poor cook.

"Where do they all run off to?" Mrs. Howell asked, and then not waiting for her husband's reply, answered her own question. "They run off to the Yankees and travel around with the army. They're like a pack of dogs living on whatever the soldiers throw them."

"I'm not sure they're any worse off with the soldiers than they are many places around here," Mr. Howell said. "At least I don't think the Yankees lock them up at night."

"Why, how can you talk like that? We'd only lock them up for their own protection. We've always treated our people well. That Clara is a case in point. We took care of her all the time she was sick. I even paid that herb woman to visit her."

Mr. Howell grew impatient. "That's the end of it, Emma. As long as I'm here, I don't want any slaves locked up at night."

Clara waited a few minutes and then feeling somewhat recovered brought the tray to the veranda where Mr. and Mrs. Howell sat in silence. She placed the tray on a table beside Mrs. Howell's chair and carefully poured them each a glass of tea.

"Thank you, Clara," Mr. Howell said, as she retreated back into the house.

Later that night in the slave quarters, Clara told Henrietta what she had overheard. Henrietta was disturbed. She had almost left the Howell plantation weeks before when the Union army was rumored to be somewhere in the vicinity. She had tried and failed to convince Clara to go with her.

"I think we should leave before that old bag locks us up," said Henrietta, trying again to reason with Clara. "The next time her husband's away, I'll bet you anything, she'll lock us up every night."

"You know, I would dearly love to leave that woman. She's the most ill-tempered person I've ever had to deal with," Clara said. "But we've been over this all before. You go, Henrietta. I'll stay here and wait for more letters."

Henrietta knew that although it had been many months since Clara had received Lottie's letter, each day she lived in the hope of receiving another. "With the war raging up and down the Shenandoah Valley, I'd be surprised if any letters come through at all," Henrietta said.

"Besides, Mr. Howell was right," Clara said, "think about a crippled woman trying to keep up with a moving army."

"You've been walking better lately," said Henrietta.

"And I intend to save my strength. When the war's over, I'm going to make my way to Fortress Monroe."

Henrietta didn't reply. She saw, as she had several times in the past, that it was useless to try and talk Clara into anything that might lessen her chances of being reunited with Lottie.

At the end of the month, Mr. Howell went to Richmond on business. "This will only be temporary," Mrs. Howell said, as Jasper herded nineteen women, children, and men into the barn. "That Union General Sheridan is close now with lots of soldiers. Everyone thinks there'll be a battle soon. You'll be safe here from marauding Yankees."

"I wonder what would happen if we refused to go into the barn?" Henrietta whispered to Clara as they went into the barn with the others.

"The missus would throw a fit for sure," said Clara.

"There aren't a lot of slaves left here to carry out her orders," Henrietta said, looking over the slaves that hadn't run away. They were mostly women with small children and old men and women, worn out by years of hard work.

"She's got the whole force of the law behind her," said Clara. "We'd end up whipped or worse." Her shoulders were slumped, and she stared at the ground. "It makes me feel like I'm no better than an old mule to be locked in the barn like this."

"You better get used to it, if you don't want to try and escape," Henrietta said.

"I wish you'd go," said Clara, knowing that Henrietta hovered on the edge of making a decision. "I'd miss you terribly, but I think you should go."

"I don't feel right about it. I don't want to leave you. You've become like a sister to me," Henrietta said, looking down at her own sturdy legs and thinking that she should have made her escape before now.

During the night, Clara and Henrietta heard the popping sound of rife fire. "What do you think is going on?" Clara asked.

"Soldiers. And they're somewhere near," said Henrietta.

The firing stopped, and the slaves went back to sleep. Clara and Henrietta woke again when they heard a rider approach. The moon had set, and it was pitch-black outside. A few minutes later, the barn door opened and Jasper came in carrying a lantern. He harnessed the gray to Mrs. Howell's trap. "What happened?" Henrietta asked as Jasper sleepily fumbled with the traces.

"I don't know," said Jasper. "Mr. Burgess just came from town. He seemed upset. Now Mrs. Howell wants her buggy." The old man opened the barn doors and led out the horse and trap. Before anyone could decide what, if anything, should be done, he had left and locked them in again.

Neither Clara nor Henrietta slept after that. When dawn broke, they heard the thump, thump of cannon in the distance. Everyone began to talk at once. "A battle's started, and it's somewhere close," Clara said amid the general turmoil.

"I wonder if she'll let us out of here," Henrietta replied.

"We'll know soon, one way or the other," said Clara. "We might as well rest while we can. There's no telling what the day will bring."

As the morning advanced, no one came to let them out. Time passed slowly, and even though the slaves sat or lounged in the hay, no one was really at ease. "I'm going to milk Blossom," Henrietta said after a while. "The children need something to drink."

Henrietta took a pail from where it hung near Blossom's stall and found the small milking stool. She bent to the task. A few minutes later, she passed around the pail of warm, rich milk. "Children first," she said, "there should be enough for everybody to have a little."

Clara hadn't realized how thirsty she had become, and she drank her share gratefully. "I wonder how long we'll be in here," she said softly to Henrietta when she was through passing around the milk.

Inside the house, Jasper was ill at ease. He had seen rank after rank of Confederate and Yankee soldiers last night when Mrs. Howell sent him on an errand. He guessed there would be a big battle in the area soon. Mrs. Howell had told him to close all the shutters on the house and to keep the slaves locked in the barn for the day. He didn't like leaving the slaves in the barn. But he didn't know what to do. He agonized over the situation as he went from room to room closing the shutters. Maybe he should free the people in the barn. If he did, what would Mrs. Howell do to him when she found out? He was in the living room when he saw the decanter, sitting on its tray near the fireplace. Maybe one little drink would help him think. Make him feel a little better. He took a little drink. Then another and another. Finally, he took a full bottle of spirits to the quarters. He drank until he passed out.

"I wonder why Jasper hasn't brought us or the animals any water. It's becoming awfully hot in here," said Henrietta some hours later when the September sun was reaching its zenith. "He's always been shiftless, but he's never been mean."

"Maybe he's left, too," said Clara.

"I'm sure the missus told him to stay here to look after her property."

"Let's try and find a place where we can see out," Clara said.

"In the loft, there's a small window," said Henrietta. "We can see the main house from there."

They climbed into the sweltering hayloft. Clara cleaned the accumulated dirt on the small square window with the corner of her apron. "It's roasting up here," she said, slumping down into the hay.

"I don't want to spend another night in this barn," said Henrietta. "And I'm concerned about the others, especially the little ones. We've had nothing to eat now since last night and only that little bit of milk."

"We'd better rest now while we can," said Clara wisely.

It was growing dark when they heard riders approach. In the fading light, Henrietta and Clara stood and looked out the small window. "Union soldiers!" Henrietta cried. "Maybe they'll free us!" Other slaves joined Henrietta and Clara in the loft and crowded around the small window.

The soldiers forced the front door of the main house and entered. A few minutes later, one came out carrying Mrs. Howell's embossed, imported mantle clock. Another soldier appeared with Mr. Howell's carved, ivory chess set in its ornate, inlaid box. "The Yankee soldiers are raiders," said Clara.

"From the looks of things, they're more interested in looting than in freeing slaves."

It was growing dark and more difficult to see. The Yankees lighted oil lamps, and Henrietta and Clara could see dim light coming through the small slats in the shutters of the house.

Inside, the soldiers continued to search for valuables. Finding no silver or expensive jewelry, they grew angry. "Let's burn this place," one of them said. "Serves those Rebels right."

"Good idea," replied a young officer with a sneer. He had come to hate the Southern plantation owners, all the people like the Howells.

A tall, gangly solider was holding a lighted oil lamp. He tossed it in the direction of the long heavy curtains that hung on one of the front windows. The globe of the lamp shattered as the lamp hit the wall, and the flame flickered and went out.

The officer removed the globe from the lantern he was holding and walked over to the curtains. He held the flame to the rich brocade, and the curtain burst into flames. He moved along to the next window and ignited another curtain. Upstairs in the back of the house, a raider set the bedding ablaze.

Clara and Henrietta watched with the others as the manor house erupted in flames and the bluecoats assembled out in front. One soldier approached the nearest outbuilding, the smokehouse, and after removing the hams, set it on fire too.

A soldier strode toward the barn, carrying a flaming fagot. "No! No!" The slaves began to scream. Henrietta looked around for something to break the window. Not finding anything, she wrapped her arm in her apron and thrust it through the small window, shattering it.

Hearing the ruckus, the soldier called out to the officer, "Captain, somebody's in there."

"It's probably slaves. Open it up. Be prepared to shoot if anybody gives you any trouble."

The barn door was barred with heavy timbers. While one man removed the timbers, the others drew their guns.

Inside, Clara and Henrietta cowered along the back wall. "Come out!" the captain yelled in a deep voice. "Men first, nice and slow, with your hands above your heads."

The slaves walked out cautiously into the flickering light of the burning buildings. The old men came out first. The women and children followed. Clara's knees were weak as she followed Henrietta out into the smoke-filled night.

"Just as I thought. Slaves," the captain said, surveying the bedraggled and frightened slaves.

"The owners must have locked them up so they wouldn't run away," one soldier said. "What will we do with them?"

"We'll take them back to the camp along with the livestock," the captain said. He turned to address the slaves. "You people are now under the protection of the Union army. We're taking you with us. We'll give you a couple of minutes to get together your belongings."

The liberated slaves looked around in amazement. Flames had reached the roof of the Howell house now, and the fire in the smokehouse crackled and popped, sending showers of sparks into the air.

Clara and Henrietta hurried to the slave quarters where they gathered up their few possessions and tied them in bundles. "I'm not sure the Yankees are any better than the Howells," Clara said as she and Henrietta joined the freed slaves assembled near the barn.

"It serves the Howells and all their kind right," Henrietta replied. "Mrs. Howell didn't care at all what happened to us. We could've been burned alive in that barn for all she cared."

Ten minutes later, they were following the soldiers along the main road. "What will happen to us now?" Clara asked, remembering that Lottie had used almost those same words when she was leaving Williamsburg. "Winter's coming, and I'm not sure I'll be able to keep up with the army," Clara said.

"We're going to where there are men. And where there are men, there has to be food. Unless I miss my guess, you'll be all set. Good cooks always find a place. Perhaps you'll take me on as an assistant." Henrietta grinned. "It's time I learned to cook."

Clara turned and gave her friend a smile and a hug. Maybe things would be all right after all. Henrietta extended her arm, and arm in arm, they followed the soldiers toward the campfire lights spread along a distant ridge.

Chapter 29
Remember Me

"I'm disappointed," said Miss Bosworth when she learned from Weza that Lottie had decided to stay at Fortress Freedom. "But I understand and respect the reasons why Lottie feels she should stay here. I am worried about her though. What will happen if Lottie's mother has never received her letter?"

Weza shook her head. "I don't know. Lottie believes her mother has gotten her letter and that she'll show up here someday."

"Did you know her mother?" Miss Bosworth asked.

Again, Weza shook her head. "I know little about her, except that Lottie has a powerful love for her." Weza hesitated. "I sometimes wonder if she's still among the living. It's a hard life being a slave, having your family taken from you, being sent among strangers."

"I've wondered the same thing," Miss Bosworth confessed, "and there is a war on." The two women looked at each other in silence, each thinking somber thoughts.

As the time approached for Miss Bosworth to return to Massachusetts, Lottie grew sad. She had friends now, and she enjoyed her time with Ned and Francine. She wasn't sorry that she had turned down the opportunity to go to school in the North. But at the same time, she would miss her teacher, and she saw the departure of Miss Bosworth as yet another loss.

"You can write to me," Miss Bosworth reassured Lottie as they waited for the steamship that would take Miss Bosworth to Boston. It was a gray December afternoon. There was the smell of snow in the air and dark clouds draped the horizon.

"I've written to Mama, but it's not the same as having her here," Lottie said. "I'm afraid I'll never see her or you again."

"It will be different writing to me. I'll write back. Through no fault of her own, your mother isn't able to do that," said Miss Bosworth.

"I can't begin to tell you how much your help has meant to me," Lottie said.

"Teaching here has been difficult," said Miss Bosworth. "I hope I've made a difference. And even though I've seen my students make progress, it has often seemed like I've been trying to empty the Chesapeake Bay with a teaspoon. If it hadn't been for you, Lottie, I might have given up during my first months here."

Lottie felt her face flush with pride and embarrassment as her teacher continued. "So many of my students were needy, and there was so little I could do to help. I felt overwhelmed by the dirt, the poverty, the ignorance, and the sorrow of the freed slaves. It seemed that what I could do for them wasn't enough. I couldn't give people jobs or all the clothes and food they needed. But I could get glasses for you and help you learn to read. You learned faster than the others once we got your glasses, because you really wanted to learn. Sometimes students think that teachers like smart students best. It's not true. Teachers love the students who want to learn, whatever their abilities. So you see, Lottie, you have meant a lot to me too."

Miss Bosworth smiled her warm smile. Lottie found it difficult to imagine that she had ever thought her teacher mean. "I've arranged," her teacher said, "for you to go into the upper school for more advanced students. Miss Forbes will be expecting you on Monday."

"I'm not sure I'm ready," said Lottie, pleased at Miss Bosworth's confidence, but already wondering if she would measure up.

"I'm sure you are," Miss Bosworth said in the tone of voice that invited no more comment.

Just then, Weza arrived at the dock, carrying a package wrapped in brown paper. She had been up since dawn, making a lunch for Miss Bosworth's journey. She had splurged yesterday and purchased white bread and a chicken to make chicken sandwiches. "I've made sandwiches for you," she said, as she handed Miss Bosworth the package.

"Why, thank you, Weza," said Miss Bosworth. Just then, the whistle blew for people to board the steamer. Lottie helped Miss Bosworth carry her bundles on board. And then the whistle blew again to signal that the ship was ready to depart.

Miss Bosworth pressed a small package into Lottie's hands and then gave her a hug.

Lottie thanked Miss Bosworth and scampered down the gangplank, moments before it was taken away. She stood on the shore watching the ship leave the dock. She did her best to smile as she waved at her teacher. She stood with Weza for several minutes watching the ship grow smaller. Then Lottie opened the package. It was a book with a blue cover. She had never owned a book. She read the words inscribed in gold on the cover, *Poetry of the American People*. She opened the flyleaf and inside Miss Bosworth had written in her beautiful, scrolling penmanship, "Remember me" and signed her name. Lottie held the small treasure to her heart. She would never, ever forget Miss Bosworth.

Chapter 30

Rastus in Tears

"The Confederates are retreating from Richmond, and there is fighting in the Shenandoah Valley where Winchester has changed hands seven times," Lottie read. She put down the newspaper and sighed. "It is hard to believe it's 1865, and the war's still going on. It seems like the war has been going on forever. I'm not sure I like reading the newspaper. It seems I'm always reading bad news about Winchester."

"I know you worry about your mother," Weza said. "But I like to hear you read about the Union army winning battles."

"There's been so much fighting near Winchester, I can't help but wonder if Mama is still there," Lottie said.

"There's no telling what has happened to the slaves in that area," said Weza. "She still may be with the Howells or she may be with the army. There's no telling."

Lottie picked up the paper again. "Federal forces have secured the—" Lottie's reading was interrupted by a loud knocking at the door.

Lottie put down the paper and hurried to see who was making such a racket. When she opened the door, Ned bounded in. "General Lee surrendered! At Appomattox Courthouse!" he blurted out. "The war is all but over!" He grabbed

Lottie and danced around with her in a dizzying circle. "Hurrah for the Union, hurrah for Abe Lincoln!"

Ned tried to induce Weza to join them. She had liked Ned ever since he had rescued Lottie from Sag and Rafe. Now she waved him away with a broad smile.

Lottie was laughing when Ned stopped whirling her about and she regained her seat. "Oh, Weza," she said breathlessly, "it's hard to believe that I'll be seeing Mama again soon."

"It'll take a while for things to wind down," said Weza. She didn't want to dampen Lottie's excitement, but at the same time Weza felt it best for Lottie not to have unrealistic expectations.

"There's going to be a celebration tonight in the tobacco barn. Won't you both come?" Ned asked.

"Lottie, you go with Ned. I'll be along later."

Lottie and Ned went out into the April evening. Dogwoods were in bloom again, and everywhere the white blooms stood out vividly against the darkening sky. "I'll be seeing Mama, soon," Lottie said happily.

There was a boom and then a flash of light. "Fireworks down by the water. Come on," Ned said. He took Lottie's hand, and they raced toward the wharf.

The following Saturday, the day was cold and wet. "Tomorrow's Easter Sunday," Weza said when she and Lottie were finishing their breakfast. "Come along to the market with me. It's too miserable today to wash. You can help me carry things."

"I'd like that," said Lottie. "Everywhere we go since Lee's surrender, it seems like a celebration."

"We'll get something special for Easter Sunday. Maybe some ham," said Weza.

As they walked toward the market a few minutes later, Lottie felt hopeful. The war was just about over, and the heavy rain that had fallen during the night had stopped. Everything smelled fresh as if it had just been scrubbed.

As Weza and Lottie drew near the market stalls, they knew immediately that something was wrong. People were standing around in small groups, talking quietly. And even though it was still early morning, the vendors were packing up their produce, eggs, and meat.

Lottie and Weza looked around for someone they knew. Lottie spotted Rastus, standing with his battered top hat off and held reverently over his chest. His head was bent, and tears were running down his face. Weza and Lottie walked over to where Rastus stood forlornly by his mule cart. Lottie had never seen a man cry unashamedly in public.

"Rastus," Weza asked with concern as they came up to him, "what's the matter?"

"President Lincoln's been shot," he said in a shaking voice. "I wish it had been me instead. I'm a worthless old man. I've lived my life."

"Is he...dead?" Lottie asked, taken aback.

Rastus nodded. "He was shot at Ford's Theater. A Southern sympathizer gunned him down," he said, struggling to control his sobs.

Lottie found it hard to believe. "Are you sure he's dead?" she asked.

"Yes. Everybody's talking about it."

Lottie was stunned. She thought about the time she had seen President Lincoln and about how he had freed her people. His kind, worn face was fixed in her memory. She felt a wave of grief pass over her. She had lost Mama, and now she felt like she had lost the one person who would restore Mama to her. Tears sprung to her eyes. Five days ago, with the news of victory, reunion with Mama seemed certain. Now along with her overwhelming grief, Lottie felt scared. What would happen to the slaves now that Lincoln, their liberator, was dead?

Lottie turned to Weza, and she was momentarily frightened by the look she saw on Weza's face. Her confidence and strength had sustained Lottie through their long ordeal. Now for the first time Weza looked tired, defeated, old. "I feel like I've lost a brother or a father," Weza said.

"I know," said Lottie. "I feel the same way."

Chapter 31

In Mourning

In the days following Lincoln's assassination, everywhere Lottie went, she saw people wearing black armbands or badges with black ribbon surrounding a likeness of the president. "Please, Weza, could I get one of the Lincoln badges?" she asked on Saturday morning. "Francine has one. Her mother bought it from Mr. Meyer. They cost fifteen cents. I know that's a lot of money for something we don't absolutely have to have, but I'd like to have one as a memento."

Weza considered a minute. All the freedmen and women were grieving for President Lincoln. She felt terrible herself whenever she thought about him. But in her long life, she had endured many painful sorrows, and little by little she was regaining her former balance. However, Weza sensed that for Lottie, the president's death was a personal blow. She went to the loose floorboard under which they kept a fruit jar with their meager savings. She took out the jar and counted out fifteen cents.

"Oh, thank you, Weza," said Lottie, looking happier than she had for several days.

A half-hour later, she brought home the badge. "I don't think I'll wear it," she said. "May I have a pin?"

Weza bent down and drew a pin out of the hem of her skirt where she still kept pins and needles. "Where are you going to pin it?" Weza asked.

"I'm going to pin it up over the fireplace where we can see it every day," said Lottie. "If I wear it, I won't be able to see President Lincoln."

Lincoln mourning badge

Courtesy of Roger Norton

Monday after school Francine was waiting for Lottie. "I heard yesterday in school that all the freed slaves are going to be shipped to Africa," said Francine as she fell into step beside Lottie.

"I hope not. I told Mama I'd stay here until she came," said Lottie, feeling more distressed than usual. She walked on in silence with Francine until they came to the road that led to Slabtown.

"I've gotta go," said Francine. "I told my mama I'd look after the little ones while she did some errands."

Lottie waved a half-hearted goodbye to Francine and hurried home. Weza knew as soon as she saw Lottie that something was wrong. She put down her washboard and dried her hands. "What's the matter?" Weza asked.

"I'm afraid of what will happen to us," said Lottie her voice breaking. "President Lincoln was our protector. Now he's dead. Francine told me that all the freed slaves are going to be shipped to Africa."

"Those rumors are nonsense," said Weza.

"But Weza," said Lottie, "if someone can kill the president, anything is possible."

Weza said nothing. She knew what Lottie said was true.

When Ned came to see Lottie the following week and found that she wasn't at home, he approached Weza. "What's going on with Lottie?" he asked. "She's not herself. Every time I've come for her lately, either she's not here, or if she is, she doesn't want to do anything. Has she found other friends?"

"Sit down for a minute, Ned," said Weza. Ned sat on the bench near the table, noticing that for once Weza wasn't working. When he had come in, she had just been sitting by herself. "Lottie hasn't found new friends. She goes off by herself. I think I know where she goes."

"And where's that?"

"She goes to a stump where she sits and watches freed slaves arrive from the North. She's looking for her mother."

"I'll keep her company," said Ned. His face lit up, and he smiled brightly.

"No, I don't think that's a good idea. She's grieving for President Lincoln and for her mother. The president's death has made her think that she'll never see her mother again."

"I don't see how they're connected."

"They're not really, except in Lottie's mind. Through all our trials, Lottie kept alive the hope that she'd be reunited with her mother. But since the president's death, she's been different. She still keeps looking for her mother, but she doesn't believe anymore that she will see her again. It nearly breaks my heart."

"What can I do to help?"

"Give her some time. That's all anyone can do now," Weza shook her head and gave Ned a little pat on the shoulder. "She reminds me of a spindly, feeble little rosebush I tried to grow one time. I watered it and took care of it. And it bloomed. Then one day when I was off somewhere, a mule stomped on it."

"What happened to it?" Ned asked, remembering how Lottie had been skinny and awkward when he had first met her.

"I don't rightly know," said Weza. "It was still alive, just barely, when I was sold. Maybe by now, it's recovered. I hope so. And I hope Lottie will get over this."

Late that afternoon, Lottie came home after watching an exceptionally large group of former slaves come into camp. She was tired and discouraged. Weza was peeling potatoes she had gotten for supper, and Lottie sat down to help.

"I can't remember what Mama looks like anymore," said Lottie as she picked up a knife.

"Now, don't you fret," Weza said. "You forget a lot of things in life, but never your mother's face."

"Maybe she has come here already, and I didn't recognize her," said Lottie. "I've grown taller. Maybe she wouldn't know me if she saw me."

Freed slaves entering Union lines at New Bern, North Carolina. After the Emancipation Proclamation and at the end of the war, freed slaves sought the protection of the Union army.

Harper's Weekly, February 21, 1863; courtesy of Casemate Museum, Fort Monroe

"Now, now, now...what's this all about?" Weza said comfortingly. "When you see her, you'll know her. You'll know her, I promise."

"But when I close my eyes, I can't see her anymore," Lottie said.

"Has Weza ever steered you wrong?" the older woman asked, looking up from her work. "You only think you can't remember her face because you've looked into so many faces in the last three years."

"I've got a picture of President Lincoln," Lottie said. "But I don't have any of Mama. My own Mama!"

"I know," said Weza, purposely saying little in the hope that Lottie would continue to share the sadness she felt.

"I told Mama I'd stay here with you until she came, but maybe we should go to Winchester and find her," said Lottie. "I only found Bebe by going to look for her."

"We'll go later on when the roads are safe," said Weza, dreading a trip to Winchester. She wasn't worried about traveling on unsafe roads as much as she was afraid what Lottie might find there. "Besides, you told your mother you'd be here."

"I guess it's best that we wait a while," Lottie said, comforted a little by Weza's calm manner.

Lottie kept up her vigil. One wet Saturday in May, she spent several hours on her favorite stump, watching former slaves straggle into camp. By late afternoon, the rain slacked off. The road was muddy and the air heavy with moisture. Lottie's coat was wet, and she was chilled from the dampness. Yet she kept watching the bedraggled, yet hopeful former slaves, struggling along through the mud.

Suddenly way down the road, she saw two women walking; one woman limped. Lottie bit her lip. She felt like leaping up and running toward the limping woman. A number of the freed slaves arriving at Fortress Freedom were weary and footsore. On several occasions, Lottie had rushed toward some woman she saw limping, only to be disappointed. Now she feared she would be disappointed again.

The curtain of dark rain clouds that had hung over the road all day began to lift. Bright shafts of sunshine emerged from under the clouds, shining gold on the new spring-green leaves of the trees along the road. Lottie was looking directly into the late afternoon sun. The two approaching women were indistinct in the amber light. Lottie watched them as they slowly grew closer. And then she saw it. The limping woman had something pink pinned to her coat, a small cloth heart. Lottie was on her feet in a second, and she began to run.

The women had noticed the half-grown girl sitting on the stump, studying them. Mama hadn't dared to hope that the girl was Lottie. Now she stopped and opened her arms.

Author's Note

Lottie and Weza are fictional characters, but I have based their story on actual events. Three slaves seeking the protection of the Union army fled to Fortress Monroe on May 23, 1861. Their owner claimed that under the provisions of the Fugitive Slave Act of 1850 they must be returned. The commandant of Fortress Monroe, Major General Benjamin Butler, refused to return them, arguing that since Virginia had seceded from the Union, the owner was not protected by Federal law. The slaves were confiscated enemy property and would be treated as contraband of war. The three slaves were bricklayers, and they were put to work for wages at Fortress Monroe.

The word soon spread among slaves that they would be free upon reaching Union lines, and by the end of July 1861, there were nine hundred freed slaves at Fortress Monroe. Two refugee camps sprang up, one known as Grand Contraband Camp, on the site of modern-day Hampton, Virginia. The other called Slabtown, located in present-day Phoebus, Virginia. By the end of the war, there were more than 13,500 freed slaves in the area. The American Missionary Association established six schools, staffed by forty teachers, and their efforts along with other organizations such at the Freedman's Relief Society and the Bureau of Negro Affairs helped to improve conditions for the newly freed slaves.

The freed slaves witnessed many important military operations. Union observation balloons on the Virginia Peninsula ascended regularly in 1862 to determine the movement of Confederate troops. The battle of the ironclads, the *Monitor* and the *Virginia* (formerly the *Merrimack)*, took place within sight of Fortress Monroe and the lower Virginia Peninsula shores. Fortress Monroe was the staging area for the Union capture of the nearby city of Norfolk and the Peninsula Campaign aimed at taking the Confederate capital at Richmond. President Lincoln visited Fort Monroe in May 1862 to oversee military operations and rode through Grand Contraband Camp.

Wherever possible I have incorporated details of slave and contraband experiences from slave narratives, letters of the missionary teachers, and other historical sources. The lives of slaves were difficult at best and torturous at times. The separation of slave families was especially hard on young children. The experiences of some slaves included transportation south in coffles and stays in slave prisons or pens.

The freedom the former slaves found in places like Grand Contraband Camp was tenuous, and the transition to freedom was difficult. There were instances of slave dealers trying to recapture escaped slaves, and even though the Federal government, the Freedman's Relief Society, and the American Missionary Association made efforts to help the newly freed slaves, conditions were primitive. Housing was inadequate, and overcrowding often led to sickness. Jobs were hard to get, and the freed slaves who found work were not always paid.

In spite of difficulties, the plight of the former slaves was far from hopeless. Great numbers of the freed slaves enthusiastically took advantage of opportunities for education. In addition to schools, the American Missionary Association working with Mary S. Peake, a notable African American educator, opened a hospital for the contrabands. Some former slaves farmed government land in the adjacent areas. Others–like Weza in our story–found ways to earn their own living. A select few had opportunities for education in the North.

According to legend, the Emancipation Proclamation was read for the first time to freed slaves under the Emancipation Oak that still stands in Hampton, Virginia. And of great importance to Lottie's story, many families—separated by slavery—were reunited at Fortress Monroe.

Glossary

abolitionists
People, mostly Northerners, who favored the end, or abolition, of slavery.

American Missionary Association
A religious organization that sent teachers and necessities to the newly freed slaves. They established six schools in the Hampton area and some schools served as churches on Sundays.

bluecoats, bluebellies
Names that Southerners called the **Union army** soldiers because they wore blue uniforms. Soldiers of the Union army were also known as **Yankees**.

Bureau of Negro Affairs
A government agency established at **Fortress Monroe** in 1863 to aid freed slaves.

chicory coffee
Chicory is a perennial herb. Its dried, ground roots are added to coffee or used as a substitute for coffee.

Civil War (1861–1865)
The Civil War began when Southern states left or seceded from the Union and formed their own country, the Confederate States of America. The Northern states fought to preserve the Union while the South fought for independence. Slavery was one of the primary issues that divided North and South.

coffle
A group of slaves chained or roped together in a line.

Confederacy
Southern states seceded from or left the United States and formed their own government called the Confederate States of America. The new country was sometimes called the Confederacy.

Confederate army, Confederates
The army of the Confederate States of America was sometimes called the Confederate army, though it was not an official title. Citizens, and especially soldiers, were sometimes called Confederates, Southerners, or **Rebels.**

contraband of war
Property confiscated during war is called contraband. Slaves that escaped to the protection of the Union army were considered confiscated enemy property and did not have to be returned to their owners. These slaves were called contrabands or contraband slaves.

copper
A copper penny.

croup
A group of respiratory infections affecting children aged three months to five years old, characterized by a loud, hoarse cough. Sometimes the cough resembles the barking of a seal.

earbobs
A popular Southern name for earrings.

Emancipation Proclamation
The January 1, 1863 order from President Lincoln, as commander and chief, freed slaves in rebellious (Confederate) states. It was an important milestone defining the purpose of

the war and it led to the Thirteenth Amendment to the Constitution, freeing the slaves.

Fortress Monroe, Fortress Freedom
A fort controlled by the **Union army** on the southern tip of the Virginia Peninsula. Some freed slaves called it Fortress Freedom. It is now called Fort Monroe.

Freedman's Relief Society
An organization established in New York in 1862 to aid freed slaves. It differed from the **American Missionary Association** in that it was not connected to any church.

Grand Contraband Camp
The freed slave village that grew up on the ruins of the city of **Hampton** under the protection of the **Union army** at **Fortress Monroe**.

graybacks
A popular name for body lice, often a problem where standards of personal hygiene could not be maintained.

gunnysack
A bag made from a coarse weave of jute or hemp, similar to a **tow bag**.

Hampton
A Virginia city near Fortress Monroe. It was burned by the **Confederates** when they retreated in 1861. When contraband slaves sought refuge with the **Union army** at **Fortress Monroe**, a shortage of housing caused many of them to build **shanties** on the ruins of the burned city.

Hampton Roads
This Virginia seaport area was of great strategic importance during the Civil War. **Fortress Monroe** commanded the northern shore of the area when Lincoln visited in 1862.

Johnny Reb, Rebels
A name Union soldiers sometimes called **Confederate** or Southern soldiers.

kepi
A military cap with a circular top and visor.

Minié ball
A Civil War rifle bullet.

observation or reconnaissance balloons
Both Northern and Southern armies used hydrogen balloons to inspect enemy positions during the Civil War.

ordinary
An inn or a tavern where meals were served.

overseer
A person in charge of a plantation and the slaves who worked on it.

pallet
A temporary bed on the floor for a child. It is usually made of blankets and quilts.

President Abraham Lincoln (1809–1865)
Lincoln was the sixteenth president of the United States. He was the leader of the **Union army** and issued the **Emancipation Proclamation** in 1863. He was assassinated by John Wilkes Booth on April 15, 1865, just days after the surrender of the main body of Confederate soldiers.

rosette
An ornament made of fabric gathered and pleated to look like a rose.

sexton
An officer of a church who performs minor duties, like ringing the church bell.

shanties
The flimsy houses built by freed slaves on the ruins of the city of Hampton.

Slabtown
A freed slave village west of **Hampton** and **Grand Contraband Camp**. The word refers to the scrap lumber from which slaves built their **shanties**.

spoonbread
A soft bread made of cornmeal, milk, and butter.

sutler
A sutler was a civilian merchant. Selling goods from a wagon or a shack, the sutler set up shop wherever armies camped.

tow bag
A bag made of coarse, woven flax or hemp similar to a **gunnysack**.

trap
A light, one-horse, two-wheeled carriage with springs.

Tyler mansion
The summer home of former President John Tyler, tenth president of the United States, 1841–1845.

Additional Sources

Books

Burchard, Peter. *Lincoln and Slavery*. Boston: Simon and Schuster, 1999. An overview for young readers.

Engs, Robert Francis. *Freedom's First Generation*. Philadelphia: University of Pennsylvania Press, 1979. Chapter two is useful for background information about contraband slaves in Hampton.

Swint, Henry L., ed. *Dear Ones at Home: Letters from Contraband Camps*. Nashville: Vanderbilt University Press, 1966. Contains letters of American Missionary Association teachers in the Hampton Roads area, primarily Lucy and Sarah Chase.

Taylor, Susie King. *A Black Woman's Civil War Memories: Reminiscences of my Life in Camp with the 33rd Colored Troops, Late 1st South Carolina Volunteers*. Edited by Patricia W. Romero. New York: Marcus Weiner Publishing, 1988. Former slave Susie King Taylor writes of learning to read and write, being a laundress, and teaching in a freedmen's school.

To Plan a Visit

The Williamsburg Courthouse, Williamsburg, Virginia

The Williamsburg Courthouse is on Duke of Gloucester Street in the historic area of Colonial Williamsburg. For more information contact: "May I Help You" Desk, Colonial Williamsburg Foundation, Williamsburg, Virginia 23185; phone (757) 220-7644, (800) 447-8679; Internet http://www.history.org

Emancipation Oak, Hampton, Virginia

The Emancipation Oak still stands on the campus of Hampton University. Follow signs from Interstate 64 to Hampton University. Take Emancipation Drive. The Emancipation Oak is about a block down the drive on the left-hand side of the road. It is surrounded by an iron fence. Internet http://www.hamptonu.edu

Casemate Museum, Fort Monroe, Virginia

The Casemate Museum at Fort Monroe contains exhibits detailing the role of Fort Monroe in the Civil War. For more information contact: The Casemate Museum, P.O. Box 51341, Fort Monroe, Virginia 23651; phone (757) 788-3391; Internet http://www-tradoc.army.mil/museum